D1320175

THE
PORK
BUTCHER

•———•

THE
PORK
BUTCHER

•———•

David Hughes

Schocken Books · New York

First American edition published by Schocken Books 1985
10 9 8 7 6 5 4 3 2 1   85 86 87 88
Copyright © by David Hughes 1984
Published by agreement with Constable & Company Ltd, London
All rights reserved

Library of Congress Cataloging in Publication Data
Hughes, David, 1930–
The pork butcher.
I. Title.
PR6058.U34P6   1985   823′.914   84–23462

Manufactured in the United States of America
ISBN 0–8052–3984–7

THE PORK BUTCHER

The night before Ernst Kestner left Lübeck to start his journey, he was awoken in the small hours by the next-door dog.

For some reason the poor fellow had been left out in the garden. In the half-light of the summer dawn he was tensed wolfishly, whining in his throat, eyes glinting at his master Dreckel's upper windows. Then he pranced at a shut door and ran once round the house in rage or panic before swivelling back to squat on the lawn, rear his head and again launch that unnerving whimpering rhythm.

Kestner wondered if the young Dreckels inside, a well-considered accountant and a wife whom some thought too lusty for her own good, had been bound, violated, robbed, left for dead. Even murdered. The dawn, encircled by rumours of the distant autobahn, seemed even lonelier in this suburban street with the dog softly howling.

And today he was leaving for France.

Standing in pyjamas at his window, paunch on the sill, Kestner had no wish to upset anyone or interfere in a situation that was probably quite normal. He could throw a heavy object at the dog or shout; but the dog was too sad. Kestner was touched by the mooning whites of his eyes gazing up at the lace curtains.

Not long ago, when Kestner's wife was still alive, a car with a siren had woken up the wintry street. His house was surrounded by uniformed men. Evidently the Dreckels had reported to the authorities that their neighbour was beating his wife to death. But Eva was only crying out with the pain of her short illness. Kestner had laughed aloud when sitting on her bed he told her how the whole town thought he had her over his knee to teach her a lesson. He was glad that her last hours of life should be heartened by so healthy a stroke of domestic humour.

But Eva hadn't laughed. Not even his jokes had given her the will to fight death off. From the feather pillow her eyes were fixed on him in acid retrospect. Ernst missed her.

Kestner was loading his steel-grey Mercedes with care just after seven o'clock when the Dreckels drove up. His books on the war in France were tied up in tinned-food cartons, he had his two suits in wrappers to hang on the appointed hooks, a week's supply of his cigarettes was under the seat. The youngsters fell out of their car laughing, promptly sobered up when they noticed how busy he was, and came to stand, swaying, rather too close to him for comfort.

Kestner smelt the lady's hot breath in the early morning cool. He felt he had to explain, with due humour, that in his opinion their dog had been somewhat neglected. They in turn explained, smiling freely, eyes flirting with each other's bodies, that they had this minute returned from an all-night party. Their influential friends had hired the Schiffergesellschaft! All of them had held hands and danced round the Holstentor in an unbroken ring to greet the dawn!

'Ah,' Kestner said amiably. 'Youth.'

Dreckel grinned. 'So our dog is there in the garden to keep busybodies away from our house.'

'And we did not forget him at the party,' Frau Dreckel said, looking her elderly neighbour too directly in the eye. Out of her handbag, as if rummaging for even more make-up than she already wore, she took some thick slices of bread overlapped by fatty meat and a bottle of beer which her husband opened by kneeling down and cracking its neck on a kerbstone. Both simultaneously shouted their dog's name – Maxi – then collapsed into giggles, Dreckel losing his balance. Beer frothed on the cobbles. The dog growled at the gate, then, released, bounded into the street. Frau Dreckel, her armpits drenching the air with an odour both sour and honeyed, began tossing up the sandwiches to the dog, who with a leap snapped them into

6

his belly at a swallow, while Dreckel, still chortling on his knees, poured the beer between the cobblestones. And the dog began savagely drinking before it all drained away.

'What a happy family you are,' Kestner said, pleased that he had not summoned the police about the dog.

'May we ask where you're going?' said Dreckel, watching the final sandwich dive towards Maxi's dripping jaws.

'France.'

'Oh, won't that be nice,' said Frau Dreckel. Now that the effort of feeding the dog was over, her loose breasts no longer heaved.

'I haven't been there since 1945,' Kestner said.

'Wasn't that in the war?'

'You weren't born then,' Kestner said kindly, as if excusing her. The Dreckels, who were in their thirties and had no children, knew nothing of death, beyond mistaking its sounds for an old man beating his wife. Pushing himself up from the cobbles, Dreckel brushed down his party suit and looked solemn. 'We are sorry,' he said formally, 'that your wife will not be accompanying you on this visit.'

Kestner had a glimpse of Eva's eyes scorning his attempts at humour. 'Oh,' he said, 'she has gone to a better place than France. Better food and wine. Better husbands.'

Frau Dreckel uttered a brief screech of approval and a neighbour across the street knocked on a window in protest at all this early mirth. The three of them looked up, bewildered, and a nightdress vanished behind a shiver of lace. 'In Germany,' Frau Dreckel said, reaching towards Kestner with another strong dose of her breath, touching his arm, 'the husbands are the best you can find.'

'That's because our women choose them,' Kestner said, and then found himself abruptly alone with his packing, for the Dreckels, the dog sporting round their ankles, had retreated into their garden, waving goodwill over their shoulders. 'Be as happy as you can,' said Kestner under his breath.

In due course Ernst Kestner settled behind his wheel, applied the safety belt and drove southward on the busy stretch to Hamburg.

He spent this hour mentally ticking off his completed preparations as though reconstructing a crime. In effect he had closed down his life. He had locked the house and proceeded to the shop on Bruchstrasse, where from the refrigerators he had filled an insulated container with generous samples of meats of his own making: sundry tastes and textures of sausage, varieties of home-cured ham, potted pork, marinated tongue: all favourites of his, all freshly made yesterday and packed in handfuls of dry ice. There was enough to last him and his daughter a week in France, if his business took that long.

Making sure the shop was empty of all perishables, Kestner had switched on the burglar alarm, locked the door, pulled the grille across the narrow frontage, padlocked it, placed all the keys in a canvas-lined envelope and addressed it to himself for collection at the main Post Office in Altona. He was too well known to use any address in Lübeck. Up to the last minute he had behaved normally with customers, acquaintances, wholesale suppliers at market, not wishing to disappoint them before he need, being in any case unable to tell them the truth. Now he had simply put a sign in the window announcing that he was closed for staff holidays. He had mentioned France to nobody except the Dreckels, and that was to show himself that he no longer cared who knew. As of today there were to be no more secrets from anyone. He had taken the plunge.

At Hamburg, having delivered his packet of keys by hand to the Post Office, Kestner turned westward with a shiver. His palms were sweating, they slid on the wheel. To reach Paris, where his daughter Tina lived with her husband Henri, he had decided to spend two days sweeping down through Belgium in the ironic wake of German armies long defeated, pausing only at Valenciennes, just over the frontier, to change his car for one made and registered in France. Yet was this elementary precaution wise or necessary? Up to Bremen he smoked seven cigarettes. He was now counting them. He tried to concentrate on the facts he had ascertained about hiring a car in France, the basic cost, the free mileage, the extras for insurance, but he was very hot, his scalp tingled. In his lungs he felt nothing.

Last week Dr Rydbeck had stated that it was not likely to be cancer. There was a growth, but one must hope that it was not cancer. It was true that people did have cancer, very true. He must enter hospital for tests. A date was fixed.

Kestner had been smoking up to forty cigarettes a day since the middle of the war. He considered tests a waste of time, if only because for a whole week he had enjoyed a unique, almost warm sense of being the first person in history to be threatened by imminent death. He seemed to have no fear or feeling of the disease itself, as if it were already as familiar as breathing.

But now he had sweaty hands and anxiety in the hollow of his stomach. He was on his way to France. Between Bremen and the Belgian border, where he would show the first passport for which he had ever applied, Kestner set his mind to a favourite pastime, the mathematics of intake. He was now 64. Since 1939 just over 28,000 litres of good German beer had passed through his body, leaving behind, according to Rydbeck, a liver in the prime of condition. He had sampled wine only on special occasions to please Eva, a maximum, say, of seven hundred bottles. By now his consumption of red meat, excluding his adolescence which he had long forgotten, must have topped 19,000 kilograms, which was, at a guess, roughly two hundred times his own body weight. Herds of cattle had been driven into him by the immensity of his appetite, porkers by the score had trotted obediently between his teeth. Kestner grinned. He had also consumed shoals of herring, while entire potato crops had been lifted to fatten his belly. What it was to have humour! Kestner grinned again, patted his stomach bulging against the wheel, and once more wondered how interesting it was to die and whether they would kill him in France.

But cigarettes, oh, cigarettes! In the course of those years, lying in bed, slipping to the back of the shop, out in the street,

9

watching television, sitting on committees to improve the town's amenities, serving as a private in the Wehrmacht, advancing, retreating, boiling a juicy ham, stirring pickles, living on and on as Hitler changed into Adenauer who had become Willy Brandt who turned into Schmidt, recovering from Eva's one infidelity, awaiting the birth of his daughter, walking home from church, at baptisms, weddings and funerals, and once, in bed, in France, in 1944, at Lascaud-sur-Marn, at dawn, in spring, the one and only time he specifically remembered lighting a match, drawing the delicious smoke into his lungs as he felt simultaneously the stirring of love in his guts, yes, in the course of all those years he had smoked – what was it again? – 864,756 cigarettes. Almost with satisfaction he now lit another, as he drew up at the Belgian frontier and a guard irritably flapped smoke away from his face with a clipboard and waved Kestner on without even glancing at his name or likeness.

In Belgium the fear grew, not of death by smoking, but of the next frontier. For fear of France he hardly saw Belgium at all. It seemed to exist below the level of the road pouring ahead of him, a land flattened by the pounding of lorries in his ears. Huge signboards offered place-names like Ypres where Kestner's father had died in 1918 a few months before his birth. Kestner tried to think of another game to keep him from racing home in retreat to open everything up with the same old keys, but instead he thought of that girl in France in 1944. He saw the shape of her haunches – she slept on her front – outlined against the window that gave on to the square of the small town where you could smell the bread baking just as the sun rose behind the church and an old woman was coughing in the attic of the next house, probably from cigarettes. Dogs barked. He saw and heard it happening, the girl's smile opening into mischief as she came out of sleep, as his heart lurched at the signs that pointed to the frontier with France.

He spent the night this side of it, in a newly built motel.

Kestner offered a pleasant smile to the French police who directed him coldly into their country. It had not been thus when last he passed this way. He had not been smiling. They had not been there.

Nothing disturbed him at first. The land was as featureless as at home. But then roadside trees began to swish their rhythm past his ears and old feelings began, the summer trees in their insistence as soft as remembered gunfire, pumping so hard into his memory that he had to slow down. Then there was a town, not in any way like Lascaud-sur-Marn, but nonetheless a French town, with badly arranged streets, a boulangerie open, and Kestner had to stop for petrol at a garage that smelt of tired oil and yesterday's sweat.

A garage too had been under the girl's window. She stirred in her sleep when they opened for business. Fumes of petrol hovered in a rainbow shimmer of volatility under the trees that overhung the bakery below. Someone that early was always making coffee. They had coffee in that part of France in 1944 when at home people were drinking swill.

While the man was filling his Mercedes, Kestner walked over the street to the bakery, with a tingling sense that the girl would call a warning from her upper window, and bought, in his bad French, a *croissant*. 'Deutsch?' the woman said, passing his wrapped *croissant* across the counter, taking his coins. And it was then, sniffing the burnt buttery smell for the first time since he last saw flakes of this delicacy adhering to her lips, that Kestner realised that one crucial element in his journey, otherwise so well planned, had slipped his mind.

He had not, as intended, exchanged his vehicle on entering the country for one of local registration. He had clean forgotten.

So he wasn't hiding.

He walked back to his own car in a daze of pride. With a chirpy laugh the attendant said something in German which Kestner failed to understand. The fellow was as young as Dreckel. Kestner perceived then that, whoever he was, he was welcome here; time had passed, old scores were settled, history had been shredded by the cutting edge of the present. Nobody in this tiny town with its funny maze of streets minded that he had come to France, if he spent his money and knew a word or two of the language. At that moment, just climbing back into the car, Kestner felt with a rush that he had been forgiven his sins. His eyes filled with tears. He wanted to sit among the old boys in the bar across the square and tell them he had an inoperable cancer and add a bottle or two to his intake of French wine.

Instead he drove on to Paris, according to plan, too upset to pin down the sources of his emotion. With difficulty he swallowed down the *croissant*, dangerously, one hand only on the wheel, envisaging the grease on the girl's mouth, with a spasm of desire pulsing between his fat thighs.

Kestner's view of Paris, formed by propaganda at the high point of the war, was of spacious boulevards down which troops marched in good order while a few civilians watched from the pavements. He had not brought his mind up to date to allow for the cruel speeds and unbelievable lack of discipline on the streets. Entering at the Porte de la Chapelle he unsteadily circled the circus three times round before the press of contrary traffic let him off in probably the wrong direction. It was warfare.

Nowhere could he glimpse the Eiffel Tower. Imprinted on his memory of that landmark, which Tina had instructed him to make for, was a photograph of the Führer on the first glorious day. In barracks at Düsseldorf, waiting to move up, the lads had tied this picture to the stove-pipe and with knives and forks hammered out on their helmets a tattoo of triumph. Kestner remembered that afternoon. It had given him his first taste of schnapps, the fiery fluid forbidden with curses by his pastor grandfather during a tight-reined boyhood in Schleswig. Now, sweating hard, part of his mind following through the game of working out his intakes (he had forgotten to count schnapps), his glance flicking upward past the lines of mansards for a sliver of the Eiffel Tower, he began to panic, fighting for his hold on humour, or just good humour, amid the really crazy behaviour of drivers clenching fists on their wheels in bouncy little cars. At every traffic-light he felt aggrieved eyes picking on his face in the big polished car or heard horns hooting behind him in a chorus of rage as he moved slowly on towards a centre that never seemed to materialise.

But suddenly, as if launched by the mounting pressure in his rearview mirror, Kestner found that he was swimming along at a good speed over a bridge, being forced to curve left between groups of imposing statuary to art and science, and then he too was proceeding at a stately pace up the Champs Elysées, as if to cheering crowds. And he had just enough nerve left – here was history, after all, unsullied by noise and fumes – to feel that he was sharing an experience common to many generations of men.

His luck held. In the same surprising moment he both saw the Eiffel Tower and narrowly avoided bumping into the backside of a bus that was advertising cigarettes. He lit up in relief, drove gently back across the river, stopped under the landmark and, while recovering, all that barracks cutlery drumming in his ears, he gazed at the enormous space where the good Adolf had once stood in sheer joy.

Tina's flat was within a few hundred metres. He decided he would never find it unless fetched. The French were a helpful people who had never done him harm. He must ask someone the way. He stepped out of the car on aching legs. Across the street, poised on a corner like one of those statues to knowledge he had just seen, stood a policeman. In his rusty French, which he had stopped using for ever in 1945, Kestner asked the way to a telephone. The officer listened to this international word with cool professional understanding, said nothing, crooked his finger once at Kestner and led him briskly to a corner café. As they entered the *patron* winked and poured two measures of pastis. Still without a word the policeman pointed the same finger at the telephone on the counter, slopped a driblet of water into his drink, and drank it. Kestner dialled.

'Tina, my love, I am in a bar with a policeman,' he said in his own language.

'What have you done?'

'I have stolen the Eiffel Tower.'

'With your criminal record it's a wonder my mother put up with you so long.'

Kestner frowned. Was this a kindly thing for a daughter to say?

'I'm alone now, Tina.'

There was a short pause, somehow denoting impatience.

'No, you're not. I'm here. Where are you?'

'In a bar with a policeman, who is drinking heavily, near the Eiffel Tower, which I can recognise from the photographs.'

'Don't move,' Tina said. 'Wait under the Eiffel Tower and Henri will come to remove the stigma of arrest from your first visit to Paris.'

Kestner put down the telephone. The *patron* was gazing at him with an upper lip curled into a grin. The policeman's expression had undergone no change. He used his finger again to indicate Kestner's glass of pastis, then tapped his own for a refill. It became apparent to Kestner that he had been lured into the most costly local call in the history of the telephone. In proper silence glasses were raised to international amity. Kestner, choking on the taste of liquorice for the first time since 1944, added a digit to his modest consumption of this filthy but heart-rending drink. He had tasted it on her tongue: that first kiss, in a back doorway, at night, in spring, when her husband was off pretending to blow up supply trains. The two men at the counter still gazed at him, as if transfixed by his generosity. He took out his savings and paid. As he left the bar, he couldn't be sure that the burst of laughter hadn't come from the television set perched high on the wall, which was showing an English film about battle at sea.

His son-in-law Henri Boyer strutted beneath the giant paws of the Eiffel Tower, embraced him nervily and addressed rapid French to him through the zigzag of residential streets that led to the flat.

Kestner understood hardly a word; it was a convention

thoughtlessly established by Henri that his wife's father, having served in France during the war, had a fine grasp of the language, and he never deviated from this error. *Bon* and *vraiment* were almost the only weapons in Kestner's hands to deflect these alien attacks on his comprehension. Panting a pace behind Henri, he ached to arrive at the apartment, which was located at the rear of a concrete postwar block in a narrow street jammed with selfishly parked vehicles. The rooms overlooked a jaded garden, a high blank wall and possibly the worst view in Paris of the Eiffel Tower, the tip of which poked above the housing of a lift-shaft.

These rooms contained little furniture made of substances other than iron, for Henri – a thin, bald, earnest fellow in whom any man's daughter might be expected to see nothing – dealt in antique hardware and had a stall in the flea-market. Mistrusting his competitors, he kept much of his stock at home for safety, and he now disappeared either to tend it or to change his white trousers which were smudged with metal polish.

'Henri's probably told you about your first evening in Paris,' Tina said, kissing her father on the lips as she had as a child. 'Business could be better for him, he has been the victim of some quite serious miscalculations lately, but he is determined to treat you well. We are to dine out, for which Henri has booked a table, then attend a concert, for which he has bought tickets, and then we shall sit outside a fashionable café, discuss what we have heard, and watch a lot of pavement artists trying to entertain us without the help of talent.'

Kestner received these remarks with deep pleasure. He had missed her asperity of tone. 'I hardly deserve such elegant arrangements,' he said, 'but I look forward to them with the respect they merit.'

Tina offered him a shy smile, her first. She was often shrill, very bossy, too frank, but the smile, however brief, turned her squarish face into a good-natured maternal oval that had always touched him. The eyes were his when she smiled, but the rounded urgent honesty of the face was someone else's, belonging not to her mother, but to the girl he had known in France, in 1944, at Lascaud, that summer, a resemblance he must be imagining, though if so he had imagined it all Tina's life and most of his. His chest hurt and he was thirsty.

She said, 'I'm glad to have you here, father. It's the first time.'

'It's the last time and you won't be glad,' he said without feeling. 'I have a lot to tell you. There is something you must do for me, not as your father, but as a younger man you never met.'

'What?'

'I want to take you away.'

Her eyes cooled. 'But I thought you were staying with us?' She simpered, to keep the mood easy. 'Surely after your success in carrying off the Eiffel Tower singlehanded you'll want our help in denuding the Louvre of all those masterpieces that really belong to the fatherland. You can stuff them in your car.'

At that word Kestner suddenly remembered. He had left his car, unlocked, packed with his suits, with the ice melting and the food going off, under the Eiffel Tower. His brain, not used to functioning so inefficiently, dissolved in panic. Henri, who had been burnishing a fire-iron in the bedroom, was called upon the scene to bring logic to bear on the problem.

He listened to Tina, his smile tight-lipped. His carefully laid plans for the evening did not matter in the least, he said. No doubt even the start of the concert could be delayed for an honoured relative from abroad. On Tina's instructions he volunteered to drive the car to the nearest suitable parking-place, unload it, bring up the food in the lift, place this food in the frigidaire and hang the suits in such wardrobe space as was available, while the two blood relatives undertook the more onerous duty of telephoning the restaurant to delay the reservation for half an hour. Henri departed smartly in his clean trousers before Kestner could protest at his generosity.

In the slightly irritant silence he left behind, Tina said, 'If you do not like him, it is only because he likes me.'

'Do you love him?'

'No.'

'I didn't love your mother,' Kestner said without thinking.

'Never?'

'I made love to her once, but only when dreaming of someone else.'

'When was that?'

'Some months before you were born.'

'How many months?'

'The usual number.'

'Is that the only time you made love to her?'

'No,' Kestner said. 'But in bed I treated her like a dog.' There was a pause. 'I hope your kind husband, who is now preventing the underworld from distributing my belongings all over Paris, loves you?'

'No.'

They were standing in the kitchen. Kestner had just wondered if the fridge contained any beer. His hand, rooting in his pocket for cigarettes, stopped. There was a split second of delight in his daughter's answer, in her company – he had already come too far, said too much, to turn back – and then the fear of what he really had to say, to do, struck him, under the heart, like his love for this woman when she was a child, aimlessly growing, vocal but wordless, on beaches, running into his shop. He sighed. 'Then he should.'

'Should?'

'Love you.'

'Ah.'

'Why not?'

'I married him to keep away from you,' Tina said briskly. 'You always hid yourself from me. I wanted someone who had nothing to hide – or nothing worth hiding.'

Not quite listening to such obvious nonsense, Kestner lit a cigarette. It tasted divine; he was dying of it. This minor confession he intended to keep up his sleeve for the moment. He didn't wish her pity to interfere with the springing of his

17

more urgent surprises, which meant asking Tina soon, ordering her, beseeching her if need be, to come with him tomorrow, driving southward, to a place of which she had never suspected the existence, at least in connection with her father: Lascaud-sur-Marn. 'Have you any beer?' he said.

At that moment Henri staggered in, his face white with effort. Kestner's suits were draped in their plastic over the front of his body. Without comment he kept travelling up and down in the lift, bringing goods into the house, a delivery man executing his duties without a trace of personality. He refused all help. He rearranged the contents of the frigidaire to accommodate the cooked meats which Kestner had brought as if to register an insult to the local food. He humped up the books, which were mostly about a war he was too young to have fought. He had then finished. His dome sweated. By now he was exuding a faint rancour that was hardly distinguishable from his usual affability.

'I shall now have a shower,' he said to his wife. 'I have ruined the evening by taking so long to help your father with his unpacking. We shall have to hurry our meal, which is unforgivable of me, in order to arrive late for the concert.'

Kestner stared at these incomprehensible words – they sounded friendly – issuing from the narrow mouth. He smiled encouragement.

'What is more,' Henri said, thereby delaying matters still further, 'we shall be unable to discuss the recital over our drinks at my chosen café, for the simple reason that we shall not have heard the music and would in any case be too hungry to think of anything to say.'

'All that is quite all right,' said Tina, mirroring his amiable delivery. 'My father expects no more than we can give him. If you can still afford it, let us go to the restaurant.'

With a sigh Henri bowed vaguely in Kestner's direction, abandoned his idea of taking a shower, and biting his thin lip waited for several moments while other residents selfishly claimed the lift, before ushering his relatives into the hot stuffy box, where he rolled his eyes upward as if to avoid confronting their disappointment in his efforts.

Forty minutes late the evening proceeded more or less as planned. Their table in the busy brasserie was only just free and at first, cooling off, Henri rallied well. In answer to a question which Kestner hadn't posed, he expatiated on his business, how badly everyone was doing, how well he personally was handling the crisis. Meanwhile he freely exercised his right of recommending his guests to give the cheaper items on the menu a fair chance. Taking no notice, Tina plumped for *carré d'agneau* (for two persons) which she shared with her father, who hadn't understood the issues. Only Henri, by severely correcting the balance, had a dinner which sandwiched the *plat du jour* between *melon au porto* and cheese, but he threw his finances into further disarray by choosing, after long thought, a wine which Tina had in any case ordered him to order.

As the meal lengthened, Henri's social energies faded into a brooding silence. He knew no German. He sat hunched over his plate, eating at speed, a condemned man at his last supper. Unaware of his son-in-law's shadowy preoccupations, Kestner felt a twinge of pity for the man who had so rashly embraced the formidable qualities of his daughter. The lamb was tender and delectable.

'What do you want me to do for you, father?' she said.

'Come away with me for two days.'

'You know I can't do that. Look at my poor husband. He's as jealous as a rat. The way he eats make me sick. But he would like to consume me just like that. He has an enormous appetite, it's never satisfied, sometimes he has to beg me for more – he goes down on his knees for it.' Tina giggled. 'When another man looks at me, up comes one of his uncontrollable rages, and they're quite exciting.'

Astounded by these revelations, Kestner glanced covertly at his foreign relative, who was stuffing fatty lumps of *plat du jour* into his mouth. A pallid sauce dripped off his chin. Wine gurgled across his palate. It felt audacious and also repulsive to be listening to Tina lightly discussing her powers as a sexual object, and his surreptitious glance now passed to her. Her hefty breasts were unsupported under a black sweater. Her mouth was full and glistened pink with a touch of saliva. For the life of him, nonetheless, he couldn't see how pottering off on a jaunt with her father could inflame Henri's exaggerated gallic passions. Then his mind jumped briefly to Jeanne, not a detail of her body forgotten, and how his own young body had melted at the thought of hers, how hatred of her absent husband had made his thoughts itch to hurt, even maim, perhaps kill him. Kestner's body stirred to pleasure under the juicy influence of this lamb and the unaccustomed wine caught in his throat. He always called her Jannie.

Again he turned to Tina. From his wallet Kestner withdrew a newspaper cutting, brown at the edges, and with his thumbnail indicated the name of a place under the headline. 'Have you heard of this town, my love?'

'Of course, I –'

'Don't speak it aloud,' Kestner said hastily. Henri would certainly know of it; nobody in France could be ignorant of, or impartial to, the existence of that town, at least in name. 'What do you know about it?'

'It was famous during your war, wasn't it? You're making me feel inferior. So don't ask me. This isn't a television quiz, father, and I'm not here to win prizes.'

'Think a bit,' he said urgently.

'It's always a mistake to think when you want to remember something,' Tina said. She looked at him slyly, lips pursed, trying to fob off his seriousness by flirting with the questions. 'Wasn't there a great big battle there? Did you win it or something?'

After a pause Kestner said, 'I was present.'

He spoke with great difficulty. In all those later years, when the scandal broke over Europe with the aridity of another war, and bitter enquiries started and the search for witnesses and the vilification, when he daily expected quiet men to stand waiting at the back of his shop under the suspended carcases until the last customer was served, then mutely handcuff him and lead him away to questions and execution, yes, when he lay awake at night, Eva next to him sharing but not sharing the sweat of his bed, and thought without conscience but with an unconscionable perplexity about that afternoon, in the heat, in France, in a town that had taught him what happiness was, in 1944, ever since then he had told nobody, not a soul, of his part in the immensely publicised and exploited events at Lascaud-sur-Marn. And now, at death's door, he was beginning to tell his daughter, and it tasted like cowardice. It was human to run away from the future; we all did it if we could. But only a murderer would run away from the past.

Kestner became aware that a suppressed drama was occurring at the table. A folded sheet of paper, not unlike a newspaper cutting, had been placed before Henri by the management.

'Thanks to a combination of bad service and my weakness for enjoying at leisure one of the rare meals I can afford in a restaurant,' Henri was saying, wrestling with his wallet, 'our honoured guest will almost surely have missed the Mozart which begins the programme. Nor will there be any taxis because the Metro is doubtless on strike.'

Kestner smiled tolerantly at his son-in-law.

Tina said, 'You are behaving like a lout.'

'No,' Henri said, fingering some soiled notes and glaring at the bill again. 'I am conducting myself like a Frenchman. Some people might be offended if, after laying on a grand and expensive dinner, their close relatives spent the entire evening conversing in a foreign tongue while hardly noticing the impressive vintage offered by a not ungenerous hospitality.' He counted out the notes once more. 'I, however, am not offended,' he added.

A waiter hovered, eyes fixed on the potential magnitude of the tip. Kestner, watching this heavy play with banknotes, which seemed to last as long as the classical andante they might well be missing, suddenly realised that he might help. He fetched up his own wallet, slipped the cutting back into it and produced his nest-egg, which was so fat that it distended his grasp.

'Please,' he said, offering Henri a symbolic portion of his life's savings.

Henri's glance, stupidly desperate, alighted for a second on the insulting bundle of notes of high denomination. His mouth twisted into a brave sneer intended as a smile. 'There is no need for you to intervene,' he said. 'You are my guest.'

'Really?' said Kestner in his comfortable few words of French. 'Good.'

They were late for the recital, which took place at the Salle Pleyel. In the taxi, a tumbril creaking them towards Henri's lethal dose of culture, he said, 'The music, if any should remain, is all German.'

'Good,' said Kestner, already worrying that he had told Tina too much too soon.

She was untypically silent. Just as oddly she was holding her father's hand under her thigh, holding it tightly, her nails in the ball of his thumb. Her message, if any, was hostile. She must suddenly have recollected the incident for which Lascaud was famous.

Now, in a corridor, they were waiting to be admitted to the music. As if in memory, a faint version of the last movement of Mozart's Dissonance Quartet seeped through the soundproof doors of the hall.

'Even if somebody has taken our seats,' Henri said, still recovering from financial setback, 'you can hear that it is finely played.'

'Really,' said Kestner, knowing that Tina's eyes were on him as if he had committed a crime.

Had he committed a crime? His dear wish was for her to tell him in all honesty yes. Or no. Didn't she see that there was nobody else to ask?

They took their seats in time for the Beethoven. Kestner had been taught at school to look upon it as his almost national duty to admire the work of this composer as an expression of his own spirit. But now, out of his element in France, Beethoven passed through several quite hectic and then piteous states of mind without altering either the tension between the three of them or any of their differing moods. Tina remained dreadfully quiet, breathing only to exhale anxiety, a fear perhaps of what her father hadn't quite said. Henri looked with petulance at the dithering instrumentalists, his bald head still agleam with the sweat of having missed the Mozart. And Kestner felt stealing upon him the beginnings of a sorrow which he had no means of judging for himself or explaining to anyone else. Yet to face that sorrow, if sorrow it was, had been his reason for coming to France, and here was the old master trying to fleet him back into Germany on the wings of energy, triumph and pride.

In the interval, to ease which Kestner bought glasses of cognac which nobody finished, he asked what the final work was to be. 'You will hear, I think, a tragic piece by Schubert,' Henri said, with Tina drily translating, 'which we can discuss together when afterwards I take you to one of my favourite cafés here in Paris.'

Kestner thought later that he survived that quartet only by spending all four movements wondering how he was managing to sit through it. The title alone seemed to bring guilty or lonely tidings: 'Death and the Maiden.' Each jagged chord, every flight of the violin, thickened the lump in his throat. He thought of his own death as already experienced, now boring; the melodies were floating him beyond it. Yet the maiden he had known, so harmonised a creature in both the address of her body and a mind that gazed upon life without prejudice, was still alive in him, perhaps the only thing that was: she used to gorge honey off a spoon, so that he wouldn't taste the pastis on her tongue, and for every day that spring, easing into their private summer, they had communicated only in such unmistakable actions, for neither spoke more than a few syllables of the other's language. He knew that she was still young, because he felt her in his old body, which had never given itself up to any other person. And then everyone was clapping, rising to the occasion, filling the halls of his brain with applause as explosive as an attack, while the four men in tails shambled back on to the stage with their instruments. And Henri, bringing his elbows into play, was hissing, 'Push, push along the row, hurry, we don't want to arrive at the café and find it is closing.'

Edging down the row, people still clapping close to his face, Kestner whispered over his shoulder, 'Come with me tomorrow, Tina,' as if he might have no other chance to speak to her alone. Out of the corner of his eye he saw her nodding. 'Is it really a matter of life and death?' she said. And he nodded back vehemently. When they emerged in the street ahead of much of the audience, Henri was so relieved that he hailed a taxi: however expensive, the depth of culture that characterised modern Paris was up to schedule at last, despite barbaric attempts to thwart it. His elbow even dug Kestner in the ribs. 'I expect you need a drink,' he said, as if he himself had already had too many. Tina looked with equal scorn at her husband and her father. 'I shall tell him,' she said coldly, while Henri paid, 'that we are visiting my mother's grave to offer our respects to her memory.'

The pavement outside Les Deux Magots was busy with fire-eaters, troubadours and acrobats. A church tower stood murkily in the background, in a film-set semblance of ruin. Kestner heard vague screams from an upper window down the street. Fumes rumbled out of the backs of buses. Whenever Henri, now tardily expansive over a second glass of bénédictine, reached the verge of pinning down what he had thought about the performance, he found a hat pushed under his nose, inviting contributions. His geniality on the wane, he kept delving into his pocket for centimes. Tina, who usually liked to contest her husband's views, kept her eyes steadily on the darkened church as if waiting for it to divulge an eternal secret. With a humour that hovered close to compassion Kestner watched the idiots on the pavement in their funny outfits trying to make a life out of making a living off the fringes of other people's luxury.

'I cannot say that it was perfect, because it wasn't,' Henri was saying as he sipped on, 'but compared with other interpretations which I have attended, there was much merit in what I heard tonight.'

At this stage it seemed not to matter to Henri that his was the only voice in the controversy he had invented or that his two companions had made up their own minds, but about something other than the food, the music, the night out.

'What did you tell Henri in the end?' Kestner said.

They were passing Orly on the autoroute south. A landing plane abruptly dominated the windscreen, tore into their ears, then faded out. It was the first time either had spoken since Henri, already late to open his stall in the flea-market, had with pained courtesy, as if in the grip of a hangover, repacked the Mercedes with Kestner's goods and found room for Tina's suitcase, which contained little more than minimum changes of clothes: mostly black, even the underwear, out of respect for her mother. Kestner noted few signs in Henri of the uncontrollable rage Tina had mentioned. On the contrary he seemed, though suffering from migraine, glad to be rid of any further potential expense, perhaps because Kestner had left him the German food in the fridge.

'I lied to him,' Tina said. 'That's the first time and I hope the last. To someone you do not love you owe at least the truth.'

'But not to people you love?'

'That would be a nice luxury.'

'May I try?'

'If it doesn't take too long. Truth is usually rather boring.'

'A few years before you were born,' Kestner said with care. 'I paid my first visit to Lascaud-sur-Marn . . .'

'Close your window. I can't hear you.'

Kestner pressed a button. Two cars raced past. The window slowly shut tight. His ears throbbed. Cold air whooshed from a vent beside the steering column. They were enclosed in the car, and it struck him that never had he been so alone with Tina, or indeed with himself, or perhaps with anyone except in an enemy's bed on that first visit to Lascaud-sur-Marn . . . It was almost as if he were about to repeat his part in the whole deadly business, rather than merely relate it.

'Take the Orléans exit,' Tina said. 'That's the quickest way to Lascaud. I looked at the map.'

'I thought we might stop somewhere and have lunch and talk.'

'Let's get it over.'

'There's more than you think.'

Tina groaned. 'Just tell me, father – don't put it off, don't make me dig my nails into your hand again, or tell lies to my husband, or not hear the music, or fail to taste good food and wine, or remind me of what it was like to be a child with a father as soft as you smooching all over me – just say it. I don't care what you've done. You killed my mother? All right. That's between you and your conscience and I'm not going to call the police, though I'd like to know. You shot a Frenchman or two in the war and you can't bear it because I'm married to one and, having once got the taste for it, you want to shoot him? Fine. But cut out the shit, eh? Just tell me about this little summer holiday of ours, however horrible it's going to be, and then I can start enjoying myself.'

A minute passed, a mile of patchy fields, factories, hazy horizons. Then Kestner said quietly, 'It's a very simple story about a young man hardly twenty-five years old. He was in the prime of condition . . .'

'Is this young man you?'

'Yes.'

'Then say so. Don't tell me a story, father. Stories always send me to sleep.'

Kestner smiled. 'That's exactly why I used to tell you stories, do you remember?'

'No, you told me stories so that you wouldn't have to talk to me. For you, life was always either a fairy-tale or a joke. That enabled you, for years and years, not to live it.'

'Have you recently taken a course in psychoanalysis?' said Kestner gently.

'Is that another joke?' By now they were out of the suburbs, the route curving ahead of them into forest. Tina reached out and touched her father's knee. 'Don't worry,' she said. 'I'm only being hard on you because I'm afraid of being soft. Go on with your – '

'Story?'

A simultaneous similar grin.

'Account,' said Tina.

'All right, whatever you thought later, I was never a Nazi,' Kestner said. 'But I did believe, we all did, that Germany was engaged in a creative act, for which in the end the whole of Europe, perhaps the world, would be grateful. Before the war I was training – did you know? – to be a dentist, but in 1939, when I was twenty, I was called up into the Army.

'I liked that. Young men do like it, Tina. Taking orders is a form of freedom. You are never in one place long enough to catch yourself up, and you leave the difficult, awkward and perhaps nervous parts of yourself back at home, in the care of your worried parents.

'I liked what the Army did for my body too. I felt immensely well, strong, full of appetite. And a young man is proud to belong to something bigger than himself, especially if he can understand its purpose – that's an extra pleasure. The purpose was very simple then, and we all knew it. It was to conquer or destroy decadence wherever we saw it, and we were quite sure that Europe was in decay. I used to think, still believing in my future profession, that all Europe's teeth were rotten and I must extract them, however much pain it caused.'

'And give it false ones?' Tina said. 'Or just leave it with no bite?'

'I wasn't clever enough to think that far,' Kestner said wanly. 'That is another good point about the Army. There may be plenty of time to think, but there's no need for it. My brain became just a sort of mechanism for registering the pleasure I took in my body and in the freedom of being thoroughly disciplined. Then I was sent to Russia.'

'Is this really what you want to tell me?' Tina said. 'Perhaps you should write up your memoirs. They would be a bestseller and millions of healthy young Germans, instead of protesting and getting their eyes full of tear-gas, would flood into the recruiting offices.'

'Tina, I can't be hurried,' Kestner said sharply. 'I have to understand it myself.' Then, relenting: 'Perhaps I should pay you to listen to me. Would a hundred marks an hour seem an insult?'

'For that sort of money I would not only listen but talk – if you give me the chance, that is.'

Kestner smiled politely but felt the humour drain out of his mind. And the traffic unnerved him. His mouth was tacky with thirst. At home he had worked out the mileages of his journey several times and the fact was that driving at his present rate would bring them to the vicinity of Lascaud-sur-Marn by early evening. And he wasn't ready for that; nor, in her ignorance, was Tina. Now therefore he slowed down to a speed quite dangerous for an autoroute, stuck between immense lorries.

'I was two years in Russia,' he said, 'and there learnt the undeniable truth of what Adolf Hitler had often told us. If you looked for decadence and found no trace of it, you would be sure to find barbarity instead. And that too, when it had the brute force to stamp out the civilised world, must be punished. You know, the Russians burnt their own land, their homes, their harvests, so that we should lack even the foundations on which to build our new order. That surely must be wrong – to destroy yourself with the same savagery as you turn on your enemies.'

'Isn't that what children do?' Tina said softly.

'I don't understand.'

'I may be wrong. I have no children.'

'Do you want them very badly?'

'Yes, but not with Henri.' Her face turned aside to stare out at the swish of the forests. 'I sometimes like what happens to his penis, but never what happens in his head.'

Again Kestner felt heavy with embarrassment at the harsh mention of her private sexuality, yet touched. A slight pain twisted, then burned for a moment, under his heart. His lung?

'I still think of you as a child,' he said. Then to his surprise: 'I would like to hug the breath out of you.'

'That's nice,' said Tina.

The pain now transferred itself to his eye sockets. The road ahead blurred slightly. He lit a cigarette and said, 'Where shall we have some lunch?'

'Do we have to stop?'

'I want to have lunch with my daughter.'

'I suppose that's better than being hugged to death.'

Kestner laughed loudly in relief. He had gained some time without a fuss. With any luck they need not arrive on the outskirts of Lascaud before some time tomorrow.

They spent an hour, another precious hour of delay, tootling along the south bank of the Loire, arguing equably about where to stop. The weather was suddenly warmer, as if they had crossed an unseen frontier between north and south. Lines of poplars scintillated in the soft distance. The breeze carried wafts of the drying grasses of summer. Now and then a reach of the river, glimpsed behind a flutter of leaf and reed, floated a dank odour through the now open windows of the car.

The French luncheon lull had emptied the roads. Villages seemed shut, reminding Kestner of invasion, of fear behind every shutter, of making love for the last time in a darkened attic. Fields were lush, buttercups growing leggy over the thick sward, while geraniums tumbled from the honey-stone balconies of every passing village which either Tina or her father rejected as lacking the right mood for their lunch together.

All this grew into one of Kestner's games. The uneasiness of feeling that he was at last in the real France was relieved by the

29

comic exigencies of the search. Tina, tasting the beginnings of a liberation from that apartment and the thrusts of Henri's wit and lubricity, was making much of her gift for finding the exact place; she proudly fanned out her intuition over the surrounding countryside. The hot sun striking his body through the glass irked Kestner. He wanted somewhere cool with litres of beer on tap and not too rich a display of cuisine. Soon it was half-past one – another thirty minutes of respite gained – and Tina said knowledgeably, 'We must stop at the next place on the right. Not only will it be quite delicious, but any later the patron will have retired with his mistress for a siesta.'

Kestner obediently stopped at the next place on the right. This was a restaurant so hemmed in by lorries that they could find the entrance only by wriggling through an oily maze of high containers and cabs far above their heads. The hot little dining-room was busy, slapdash and loud. No choice was offered. They were simply brought dish after dish of food, clattered on to the table, by women with maps of sweat encircling their blowzy armpits, shouting backchat over their shoulders to regulars lounging at their ease over thin wine. Kestner, dazed by the fury of the service, the food tumultuously piling up before him, was pushed into even greater reticence, by the fact that, perhaps for the first time – no, that wasn't possible, but it did seem like a beginning – Tina was actually facing him.

She faced him across a narrow table. He could see the intimacy of her eating, her eyes now and then emblazoned with light as a departing lorry flashed its windscreen into the depths of the restaurant. And it was a mirror image: these were his own eyes, much younger, vulnerably looking at him at such close range. For a while they were too busy eating, clearing the way for the next course, to talk. A tomato salad came and went, a terrine in a crock paused on their table for a moment only to be whipped away, some crudely sliced raw ham allowed their forks just time enough to transfer it to their plates, and then, as the place emptied and quietened, the lorries outside rumbling off to let more light fall in a trance across their table, the escalopes in a tinny oval dish, encircled by ramparts of carrots, peas, potatoes, seemed to clear a space in the middle of their silence. And Tina said fondly, helping herself, 'So at last you're in France, father.'

'It's not the first time.'

'I know. But it's the first time you have come to see me.'

'Do you know why I couldn't come before? I longed to.'

'I thought it was because you couldn't stick Henri. I don't blame you.'

'No, but you hurt me very much, I think, by wanting to live here. It turned my love for you into a conscience.'

'Why?' said Tina. 'How?'

'Have some more vegetables.'

'Don't change the subject by appearing to care for my interests,' Tina said. 'You're only interested in yourself, and I don't blame you for that either. It's the most human thing you've ever shown me, and I still want to learn from you, funnily enough, but not by rebellion. I must have been an awful little girl. I hated you for not being yourself with me, even if I didn't quite know who I was either.'

'You were a splendid little girl, quite delightful,' Kestner said. It sounded false. Then the truth: 'You reminded me of someone I loved.'

'That's sentimental.'

'I know.'

'I won't listen to it.'

'I'm paying you a hundred marks an hour.'

'Very well,' Tina said. 'In that case, who was she? Incidentally, I only went to France – you always seemed so sensitive to it, though you never said much, that was the trouble – to kick you in the teeth. Oops sorry – dentistry again. But I bet you're not sorry you didn't spend your life looking into people's mouths. Of course you wouldn't have been able to smoke so many cigarettes. Hygiene, you know, father.'

'Ah.'

Kestner, put sharply in mind of his condition, felt that she was taking over the story. Perhaps that didn't matter. On the contrary, once more, following the dreadful pattern of the years, here was a chance for him to evade that story. He could let someone else ramble on, as he always had, and say not a word himself. Wasn't it kinder, wiser, to let death overtake him without easing on to others the responsibility for what he had done, that hot afternoon, in June 1944, under orders, in a town less than a day's journey from this piece of meat which he was now chewing down with difficulty? Then Tina said, bringing reality back with a nice smile, 'Who was she, then? You still haven't told me.'

'Her name was Jannie.'

'That's a good name,' Tina said with generosity. 'I wouldn't have minded being christened Jannie.'

'Don't, please don't,' Kestner said in anguish, twisting away. The restaurant was almost silent now except for the waitresses hissing gossip. 'I get so muddled that I can't talk at all.'

'You were in love with her,' Tina said, again taking over, pleased again to be deploying her intuition. And she waited. She thought she was helping. All Kestner saw was a dark void, somewhere beyond this moment in this place, a void into which he had to venture. All the lorries had gone. The slant of light beat against his eyes.

'I was in love with her,' he said. He had not said that, even to himself, all these years. 'I still am,' he added with boyish provocation, too loudly.

'Is that so difficult to say?' Tina whispered.

'Yes,' Kestner said. 'Because you have made me say it.'

The meat was finished. A hand removed the dish in a trice. A platter of cheese replaced it. 'I would like some wine,' Tina said, and within seconds a litre bottle of rouge was plonked on the table. Tina drank a glass as thirstily as water, then poured more, while Kestner in surprise noted these habits with a confused inkling that somehow his daughter was half-French, and that made him ache with a moment of loss, as if every trivial incident were in conspiracy to bring him nearer the thought of Jannie, her presence.

'Then, early in 1944,' he said, picking up the thread he had lost in the car, 'I was posted to a depot near Celles. None of us knew why, but it was probably as back-up to our forces massing in the north of France to resist the coming invasion from England. We were ordered to be very correct to the local people, to make friends where we could, to keep our eyes and ears open for the activities of the Resistance, and meanwhile to train and rest, as part of the garrison on light duties, perhaps as a reward for our long years on the Russian front. It seemed, you know, that the Führer didn't regard the French as decadent. He would so much have liked to be on good terms with them.'

'What a pity he didn't survive to see the two countries now,' said Tina drily. 'Why, they're practically lovers!'

'Yes, he was a visionary,' Kestner said with no irony of tone. 'Some people I know believe that it will take a hundred years to realise what an opportunity for rebirth Europe missed in 1944.'

'Hm,' murmured Tina. 'How often history gets it wrong.'

'Quite. But I myself had very little to do at first. It was March, I think. An early spring. I had commandeered a bicycle from somewhere and at weekends I used to push off into the countryside south of the city and explore interests which, do you know, I've never thought of pursuing since. I had a heavy pair of binoculars and the trees were still bare, but just coming into leaf, and I could lie in the cold grass and see huge foreshortened distances that were alive with birds, birds resting on branches on their way somewhere else, yes, birds caught in the act of migration, you see, north or south, because every weekend they were different – those soft little valleys were a sort of anonymous crossroads for the birds, and of course for me too, because I could be alone there and wonder what I would do after the war, which turning I would take, whether we won or lost. We still trusted that the Führer would win, even then, you know. Our cause, whatever they say now, had much good in it. Before he died, if they hadn't killed him, he would have given

33

all those countries back to themselves, but with our energy renewing their ideals.'

'You're romancing,' Tina said, draining her second glass, refilling it at once.

'Yes – or I was. I sat in little stone churches, debating when they had been built, really dying to know. How do I say it? Feeling in the stone the weight of the people who had been there before me – the generations who had created this repose I was enjoying – and who had migrated like the birds before I could get anywhere near them. Was that so romantic, Tina?'

'Yes,' she said crudely. 'It was stupid.'

'Oh, well, you're probably right,' he said. Then added, cunningly, to his own amazement, 'What I really wanted was sex – no, I mean someone to love.'

'We all do,' said Tina lazily. The litre bottle was half empty. The three waitresses, arms folded in a slack imitation of patience, were muttering together with their backs to the bar.

'I'll tell you later,' Kestner said, putting down some money.

Tina tapped the notes with a finger. 'Is this because I'm not listening?'

'No, it's for the bill.'

'Then tell me now. Later I might be sleepy.'

A hand snatched the cash off the table, in seconds returning with the change.

'And then one day,' Kestner said, 'a bit later in the spring, a day that smelt of earth and things growing, I don't know how to describe it, it had been raining, I was again lying on my belly, watching of all things a beetle crawl up and down a blade of grass, when something – a stone, I thought later – struck me on the back of the head, and I woke up locked in a shuttered bedroom – the quilt was white, embroidered, lacy – with blood still oozing in my hair, and naked. It wasn't quite dark yet. Through the window I could hear the normal idle sounds of a village in the evening, murmurs of talk like those waitresses – do they want us to go?'

'Yes, but we're not going.' Tina said. 'I'm finishing my wine.'

'Could I have a coffee?'

Nodding, she waved a hand. A machine hissed. One of the girls was humming between her teeth a recent Louis Larguier melody. The sun outside, turning away from their table, drenched the afternoon.

'I didn't know it then,' Kestner said, 'but some young boys had knocked me out, dragged me through the fields, knocked me out again, and delivered me to the back door of a man called Bernard, one of the pastry cooks in Lascaud-sur-Marn, who was off on some operation to blow up something that didn't matter to our war effort.' He sipped his coffee. 'I could smell the oil from the garage and the new bread baking next door. There was a café across the street. The tables outside were arguing, I think, about the right or wrong times to plant things. I didn't quite understand what they were saying. I gathered later, from Jannie. Somewhere downstairs she was listening tensely, in agony, to every sound from the village, straining her ears to know if anyone was even faintly aware that she had a half-dead German soldier in her bedroom, whom her husband, if and when he got back from his silly enterprise, might want to question – but probably wouldn't, the Resistance weren't interested in single hostages then, they were too frightened of reprisals – and whom in panic she had stripped naked, to stop him escaping, and hidden his clothes under hers in a cupboard. I first saw Jannie's face when she crept upstairs to see if I was dead.'

'Stop there, father, I can't bear it, I'm drunk,' Tina said sloppily.

Kestner let out a long breath and picked up his change. Outside the sun hit hard. A dusty smell of limes was blossoming in the heat of the afternoon, and as they drove out of the little place, past a bakery, a petrol station, a café dead to the world, Tina fell asleep, with her jaw dropped in a sag, her neck painfully angled. And, unfussed, Kestner quietly put his mind to the number of places which he had ringed on the map, where he and his daughter could pleasantly spend the night, before the onslaught of tomorrow.

Kestner drove on for an hour, glad that this woman was asleep next to him. Her position, skirt ruckled above the knee, implied trust. Also, having articulated so much that for years he had hardly dared allow to enter his waking thoughts, he no longer felt the burden of secrecy. Confession had aired his mind.

Not that he had ever had to think about Jannie in any conscious fashion. Perhaps because their talk was restricted to a few isolated words of each other's language, she was present inside him only as images, glaring overlit pictures which, when they occurred to him, burned out, for as long as he could hold them, all the ordinary contents of his mind. They did not even seem like memories. They had never faded at the edges. Indeed they always struck him not as the past at all, but as events both fresh and perilous which only now was he on the point of experiencing. Tomorrow he would fall in love.

At home in Lübeck, for years after the war, he had often woken up next to his wife looking forward to Jannie, to seeing her briefly on his way to the shop, briefly but with such force that he was all at once deafened to familiar voices, to the clangour of the tram grinding uphill to town, to reality. He could see her, dressed in the long black skirts that the old women wore, backed at this moment by the trusting silence of Tina's sleep. He could never explain to Tina, if she had never so loved, what such love was.

Kestner had risen with difficulty to his feet when Jannie sidled into the room. His skull ached. He had no idea what incident had brought him here, but he did not feel endangered and for some reason his nudity was of no account, as if he sensed her familiarity – having undressed it – with his young body. They tried a few words, gave up with a simultaneous shrug, then looked at each other. She gazed at him without hiding her interest in his shape and size. Her eyes did not linger on his penis but simply registered it as part of an agreeable whole. Separated from his uniform, from any rules or restrictions imposed on him, he was made to feel powerfully himself, a structure entirely human, vulnerable but strong – and unique: her eyes, even then, had the gift of conveying unemotionally the news that no such man, for her, had hitherto existed and therefore human history must consider itself to that minute extent enriched. He did not notice that she was any sort of beauty, though her eyes were large and of a deep blue and tilted slightly upward at the corners, her long hair seemed bleached by sunlight and her cheeks were firm and rounded – an apricot, peaches, the softness of a rose: he never got these comparisons right; he often tried, but in physical detail she persisted in being only herself. Her head was set well on a long neck and she had fine hands. He knew that he must be severely at risk – a German soldier in a Frenchwoman's bedroom – yet he had no impulse to escape. He wanted instead to make love to her with an ardour that bewildered him.

She knew this and he was convinced she shared it. He found such a notion beyond belief. For her the likelihood of dishonour and death in her own village must far outweigh any satisfaction she might derive from taking her pleasure with an enemy. Kestner was never to understand this frightening nerve of hers. Even now he could only think of it as love or as some manifestation of desire that aroused the depths in her only when the risks were high. On that first occasion she left him brusquely, locking the door behind her, then returned when it was dark with his clothes neatly folded. Hands on hips, grave to the point of fondness, she watched him dress; it was indeed as though they had spent the intervening hour in bed. But she had merely waited for night to fall, nicely balancing the threat of losing him to the mercies of her husband Bernard, who might return from his operations at any moment, against the possibility that by releasing him herself in secret he might report the abduction to his superiors, thus bringing down on the village an appalling vengeance. Yet Kestner knew – how? and why so certainly? –

that her confidence that she would see him again, that she had already imprisoned him in her body, sprang from the very act of drawing so dangerously tight those twin threads of risk.

In her shuttered kitchen she tapped at leisure a tumbler of cider from a barrel and offered it in charity without a smile, while conveying by glance what her smile might be like. As he drank the cider down, she flapped open a red handkerchief in front of his face as if signalling, then draped it on the inside of the window-sill and pointed upstairs. It was a touchingly crude and oblique message which he picked up at once, a child's device to tell him that if ever he happened to be passing she would leave him a sign. Then she turned off the light, another risk. He heard her gently unbolt the back door, open it – he could almost feel the thump of her heart – and let the cool outer silence flow between them. 'Allez,' she said, and as he slipped into the darkness and saw the prickling vault of stars her hand closed by accident over his hip and he was blinded by a flash of what he recognised for the first time as the stupidity of happiness.

In the car Tina was still asleep, but groaning in unease under her breath. Kestner realised he must have driven over a hundred kilometres along roads he had so often covered on the map at home. He was being drawn inexorably back – but also, he knew, forward. Though unaware of the passage of time or distance for perhaps two hours, he felt simply glad to have spent some time with Jannie alone. Once again, and as usual, those events were happening now. He had never let them become the past. They were not even preserved in the juices of his deep physical love for her. They were always present, just waiting for him to savour again the old anticipation and reach out for her, in this field or that wood, in impenetrable banks of fern above the river or in her own deep bed – the secrets of all of which had never been broken by him. Until now.

'Where are we?' Tina said drowsily.

'In occupied France,' Kestner said. 'It's the spring of '44. You haven't been born yet.'

'Yes, it feels a bit like that,' Tina muttered. 'I shouldn't have drunk all that wine.'

'Why did you?' Kestner asked with interest.

Tina yawned. 'Perhaps because you couldn't even hide from me the fact that I had the wrong mother. After steering clear of me for so long, for most of my life, you've suddenly decided to be cruel. Why's that?'

Her tone was void of acrimony. She just sounded tired.

'You wouldn't have been you, Tina, if you'd had a different mother,' Kestner said with wan logic.

'No, and you'd have been a better father if you hadn't fallen for that French biddy.'

The voice was still sleepily amiable. Kestner briefly wondered whether he need any longer even go through the motions of trying to understand women. Eva's petty misery had for years perplexed him to the depths; she had in theory far more to be thankful for than he, who had carried unspoken the responsibility for a war that had murdered his beloved. His heart tightened within him. It was the first moment of undressed fear since his arrival in Paris, and no joke that he could think of would get him through it.

'Tina,' he said, 'you will understand. I promise. You will understand tomorrow. Tonight we are going to stay together in a comfortable hotel.'

She wriggled in her seat. 'Oh, God, no, not more,' she cried. 'Can't you see that I can't take it and don't want it? Whenever you start talking, I get drunk, I keep falling asleep, I've only brought one change of underwear, I like Paris, I'm myself, I enjoy hating Henri and being done over twice nightly by his silly anger. I simply don't need any more reminiscences, I'd rather watch television.'

'Perhaps,' Kestner said with implacable kindness, 'they'll have a set in the hotel.'

They stayed the night in a small town south of Chinon. Kestner had once rumbled through this Mazarin in a lorry on his way north to the invasion front near Caen. How he had wished for death! With what dedication he intended to court it in the battles that awaited him! When the lorry was halted briefly in a pile-up of traffic that summer evening, everyone could hear to the northward the distant guns rolling in a promise of death across the hazy yellow sunset.

By then Jannie had taught him the taste for risk, the insensate nature of life without it. Enraptured by those guns, he had liked the quiet evening glimpse he had caught of the town, the sun casting almost horizontal shadows across the strictly classical lines of the seventeenth-century terraces – and now, suddenly knowing why, he liked it again. It was indestructibly ordered. It was built to a pattern of rectangular blocks within an oblong of walls. A public square graced either end. The formal streets, with their ranks of town mansions each boasting its archway into a stable-yard, criss-crossed at exactly regular intervals. You could never get lost in such a place. It had the precision of a work of art composed on scientific lines. Those who had lived there in Mazarin's ideal townscape occupied the outward form of a society in which obedience and rank were the prime virtues, within which discipline every vice could freely flourish. Kestner's own standards, he felt, were summarised by the apparent inhumanity of so human an attempt at perfection. Tina did not like it. There was no night-life except sleep.

She also refused to dine with her father unless he promised to make no further reference to his mistress. This he thought unfair, but he was living with Tina, for however brief a spell, and her wishes must be respected now if later he were to enforce any of his own. So they sat down quite happily together. She had changed her dress, he noted, and smelt of expensive shops, and they talked of Lübeck and the business in Bruchstrasse and some of the hoary or spicy old customers whom Tina recalled and which of them was dead and who wasn't, until Tina said, halfway through a thick steak that oozed juice into the crunchiest of *frites*, 'And how are you, father? You haven't said a word about yourself. I'll allow you to talk about your health for ten minutes without demanding any payment for listening.'

'I'm well.'

'No, you're not,' she said chattily, mouth full.

'How can you say that?'

'Because there's something too thoughtful about you. You look at me too hard as if you were taking a snapshot. You're not casual. You're showing me too much love – well, no, consideration. Are you trying not to hurt me? If you were my husband, I'd think you were consorting with another woman.'

'I'm not permitted to talk about other women,' Kestner said with a smile.

'You smoke too much.'

Kestner raised an eyebrow. Between each course he had lighted a cigarette. He had smoked a few centimetres of it, in ludicrous deference to belated medical advice, then stubbed it out and placed the ashtray out of sight on the floor. Once the waiter kicked it and apologised, assuming it to be Kestner's foot. With half his mind he had been toying with one of his games: how much or deeply he needed to inhale to knock up a pain in his lung. The pain never came. But he was fascinated by this insipid version of the almighty sense of risk he had shared with Jannie. Every time his lung felt nothing, he had won.

'We all enjoy folly,' Kestner said with an attempt at levity.

'I want you to be careful.'

'I'm only an old pork butcher feeding off the fat of his memories,' Kestner said lightly, beginning to worry. 'Plenty more where I came from.'

Tina ignored this. 'Men in their early sixties are very vulnerable,' she said.

'All men at all times are very vulnerable.'

She paused, fork in hand, meat on fork, sauce dripping off meat, and regarded him with steady concern. 'You've given it away, haven't you?' she said. 'No, don't reply. But I think you've seen your doctor and he told you – to stop smoking?'

'Yes,' Kestner said crossly. He had wanted the timing to be

his own. 'Just a precaution. Men in their early sixties, something thoughtful about them, looking at their daughters too hard, not being casual enough, etc. Actually he told me to consult a psychiatrist.'

'But . . .'

'Please don't go on, Tina.' He managed a grin, then took her hand. 'I want to tell you everything, indeed show you everything, as I have planned it. Now here's this clumsy waiter who keeps kicking my ashtray busy showing so much love and consideration that the least you can do is choose a sweet.'

Tina buried her face in the menu. A hand reached out to her glass of a local wine. Behind these defences her voice was slightly muffled. 'Tell me about your girl, then,' she said unevenly.

'Thank you, darling,' said Kestner. And then it was very easy. He spoke of the red handkerchief that four days later was drying on the upper windowsill with other washing as he passed, dressed in peasant blues requisitioned from a shop in Celles, pushing his bicycle between the thick bushes of a path behind her house, and of waiting until dusk and knocking gently at the back door, ready to run, and of finding her with an almost painful abruptness of passion (she somehow jarred his kneecap) in his arms, and of a bolt on the door cracking in his ear like a rifle-shot, and of her skirts being thrown up in a rustle of triumph, and of kneeling before her, all clothes and confusion, all happiness, as if he had known her for ever, on the stone flags of the kitchen floor.

He spoke too, as the dessert topped by strawberries arrived on the table and the ashtray went under, of the map of the district which she laid out on the counterpane of her bed, on the contours of which, as the weeks of spring passed, she marked so many of the spots in that river valley where they would meet, next time, next time, that even now he could draw that map from memory: every rise and declivity, every rush bed where their bodies squelched so rudely that in the transports of love they rolled over and over in spasms of laughter, every barn and byre when the backs of the farmers who owned them were turned.

And she always brought food and drink, cider that got in his throat and made him belch apples, bread only just not still warm from the bakery below her bedroom window, soft cheese made yesterday from the goats that tinkled out from the village to ravage other people's hedges, fry from the river which she burnt black over a tiny fire while he waved down the smoke with yet another of her red kerchiefs. And they spoke in single words. That was the most pagan part of the game. And it was more than enough. The communication, their dangerous community, lacked nothing. And in all their meetings, as the love grew to a pitch of just bearable obsession in weather that was relaxing daily into heat, there was always, never forgotten but lashing her to frenzies of oblivion in their sex, the icy risk: boys might pass a field away and see a glimpse of red; a farmer's horses would nose past their lair, the plough stoning them as they hid; and worst of all Bernard, coming home armed from an unpredictable hitch in his attacks on the occupying power, might catch them at climax in his own bed.

'Why did she do it?' Tina said jealously.

'Nobody liked her in the village. She was a cut above them. She wasn't interested in politics. Her husband neglected her for his beliefs – or his fun. She needed love because she had so much of it to give. That's it, I think.'

'No, it isn't,' Tina said.

'What is it, then?'

'She wanted to destroy both of you, of course. Death is sometimes the most lively thing around. She really must have hated sex.' Tina paused, a strawberry at her mouth. 'Oh, father, please don't let her destroy you now. You're a good man.'

They both slept on it.

When he awoke to fine weather Kestner felt closer to his daughter than at any time in her life. That, he supposed, had been his intention in telling her about Jannie: to make it easier for her, for them both, to bear the events that were bound to happen today, easier to enter into the shadows which Kestner could not face alone. But he was emptily content that morning, as if relieved at last of an intimacy that had burdened him for too long. At breakfast Tina noticed it at once and took credit for the purge. She had cornered him into telling the truth. In silence they sat together in the pleasant warmth outside, appreciating the bustle in the long square, the violent kick and chortle of a moped fuming the air, the men in lazy blues supporting a zinc counter with wine to their lips. As if her resistance to simple things had hitherto blocked them out, she savoured the scents of warm bread and freshly made coffee that on a light breeze circulated the promise of their comforts. There was a gentle thrill in being not quite here any longer, but already on the way elsewhere.

In the car Kestner behaved as if suitably cleansed, himself again. His manners were formal. He kept his eyes benevolently on the straights of road ahead, now and then making a favourable comment on landscape: a line of planes orchestrating the otherwise dull melody of the horizon, or a field of barley crocheted with cornflowers, or massed poppies trumpeting their colour over the brow of a hill. The sun strengthened, pressing these almost vulgar effects of nature on their attention, as they moved further south. Now meandering through undulations of farm country, punctuated by signposts that slipped past before Tina could read them, they enjoyed between silences a few tiffs over the map's inability to live up to its purpose. Once, on Tina's interpretation of the turning to take, they ended up in a dead end flapping with shocked geese. 'You goose,' Kestner cried, rocking with laughter. His nerves, yesterday so prickly, seemed to have settled. Tina felt simply on holiday, yet anxious to hang on to their closeness in case she had guessed right about the deadly result of his smoking.

In the untimed middle of the morning they reached a little town called Muriac, which from afar resembled toy bricks scattered by an indolent child over a conical hilltop. They drove up into the town, Kestner saying that he had once sat in its church, gaudily painted in slabs of baroque colour, not mentioning that on a similarly hot day, in 1944, after the events, he had cast himself down flat in the chancel on a tombstone in his jackboots in a hopeless tantrum of hope that he might be forgiven, and a priest, thinking him dead and fearing reprisal, had run for help. But now the church was locked, happily quashing yet another opportunity for Kestner to spoil, by undue reminiscence, the balance of the morning for them both.

There was, however, a market. The square, the usual small-town assembly of cafés and banks in higgledy-piggledy buildings topped by squinting dormers narrowing upwards to a clocktower with a hoarse bell that announced the quarters as if they had happened long ago, was packed with stalls that heaped up on their boards the various fecundities of this countryside, tomatoes, cheeses, hams, artichokes, cherries, every monger pricing his goods lower than those of his neighbour as noon approached, wives hustling and bridling for preferential treatment under the stripes of shadow from makeshift awnings, and at once Kestner began taking a professional interest. He was hypnotised by the massed foods, and how it touched Tina to see it! A fat terrine concentrated his eye as he mentally ticked off the ingredients down to the last subtle pinch of spice. His face grew solemn over a plump rounded pink ham bordered in black, from which slivers of meat were curling deliciously off the slicer. He gazed into the jellied depths of a brawn, nodding sagely, an old man who had devoted his working life to the manufacture of such delicacies, wondering if here in the south he had been outclassed, full of admiration but also racked by doubt. Taking his arm, without thinking, Tina squeezed it to her breast. 'Oh, do let's have a picnic,' she said. 'I don't want to sit in a restaurant with you, other people pricking up their ears at our language, and all that. Let's buy and buy and buy. We can have a feast together. By a river. Let's find a river bank, with some shade. We're on holiday.'

45

Kestner paused, stared at a galantine studded with olives which he wished he had made, and nodded agreement, with both appetite and gloom.

They shopped. They bought, wrapped in oiled paper, paper-bagged, tucked into Tina's shoulder-bag, slipped into the baggy pockets of Kestner's suit, far more food than they could possibly consume. Kestner thought of Jannie's offerings, the brief hungry respite from their acts of love, by streams, up gullies, in bed. Tina imagined the open air, the long pause of noontide under the sun, when people without conscience ate their fill and dozed in peace. The cracked bell sounded another long-forgotten quarter. The square cleared of wives as the flies gathered and the banks shut and the cafés filled; the sun struck daggers of light through glasses of white wine. And at the last moment, before everyone vanished into shuttered gloom to fall upon excessive meals and leave the afternoon to look after itself, they plunged, parcelled to the eyebrows, into a cavern of a shop and bought, at Tina's request, a choice of local vintages. They would have to eat with their fingers and drink from the bottle.

Outside the town they drove very slowly into the heat. Tina kept claiming to detect the thin blue lines of rivers on the map, but for a spell these turned out to have dried up, to have allowed cement works pounding out dust to develop on their banks, or simply to be not there at all. A succession of narrowing lanes corkscrewed the muscles of Kestner's shoulders at the wheel. An hour passed. He worried about the cooked meats sweating in their grease on the back seat.

Not for a second had he the time or the wish to imagine that within hours, or less, they would be driving into Lascaud-sur-Marn. His mind was preoccupied with the immediate irritants: a trapped fly swerving off the windscreen at his face, the lack of rivers when rivers were officially supposed to materialise, an increasing sense that the picnic was a bad idea just because it had struck them spontaneously as such a good one, a touch of indigestion from not eating on time – this a particular annoyance since it reminded him, with no discernible logic, of the state of his lungs. And then, as they curved down rather too fast into a narrow cup of valley, banked on all sides by meadows as thickly flowered as tapestries leading up to woods against the skyline, he braked so sharply on a short bridge that all the packeted food in the back shot in disorder forward on to the floor and a bottle of wine hit the seat-belt attachment with a clang.

'Heavens,' shouted Tina, her head banging the sun-visor.

'I'm not going on for ever,' Kestner said, backing up. 'Let's give it a chance. Here's your river.'

'It's not on the map,' she said moodily.

'That's why it's here.'

She was rubbing her head. 'How can an old bird like you be so impossibly romantic?'

'I've always been like that,' he said with satisfaction, turning off the engine.

Kestner stepped out of the car. He leaned over the bridge. A long way below him, screened by the scrawny branches of not very interesting trees, in bottle-green gloom, trickled at a slow pace a rivulet hardly worth the name. But it smelt cool. After the ins and outs of the journey a silence of great portent hit his ears; and then he heard crickets. All the way up the hills, all round the arena topped by gently moving trees, a buzz of insects lifted into the air, as if they had been interrupted in gossip by his loud car. A bee surged past and settled into a rising field. There was no sign of human residence or activity. The valley was busily lost in the middle of summer. After a second, with shock, he heard Tina's shoes scuffle on the gravel of the bridge. He had momentarily thought himself alone.

'Wasn't I right about the river?' she said.

'Of course I was,' he retorted.

With only a bit of argument they took up their position in deep grass above the water. They could hear its pathetic trickle. They had no blanket to sit on and nothing to eat with. But the food, over which ants soon crawled, on which a species of blond fly soon alighted, across the richness of which the faint breeze blew seeds, tasted delectable. Their fingers were now slick with drips of melted fat. Tina's mouth wetly bulged with the shape of the tomato she had just pushed into it. Their eyes ranged freely over the close limits of the landscape. The sky was blue, very blue, the blue of eyes. Kestner flipped strands of ham, cured to perfection, into his jaws, tossing torn morsels of bread after it, clutching lettuce leaves in readiness, munching, masticating, groping for the bottle and upending it between his lips. He sat crosslegged in the spindly grass, very upright, giving no thought to anything specific, just doggedly enabling the entire contents of that market to glut his system – whereupon, with a last gurgle of wine down his throat, he fell back into unrumpled grass, rolled over on his stomach with an involuntary belch, dragged an old pair of silver-rimmed glasses out of a pocket, and began staring at the even more limited horizons of the juicy green universe under his nose.

Smiling to herself – they had hardly exchanged a word – and clutching her own bottle between her knees, Tina was feeling a little somnolent. She also felt pleasured. She had forgotten Paris. A bee drowsed past, paused, head in flower, nuzzling, then noised away into silence with the sad murmur of a distant vehicle. This was the high point of her holiday. Obviously her father wanted nothing more than to have shared, on his own terms, the secret of his love with her, and now, too soon, they could both move off back to their separate homes, loving and understanding each other a little more perhaps, probably for the last time. Almost falling asleep, she felt a surge of the essential disappointment of happiness; it led to nothing.

Then Kestner, his voice growling out of his belly because of the boyish way he was stretched out among the grasses on his front, said, 'Look, Tina, just look. They're all running up and down this plant. What is this plant? I almost remember. It's got a hairy stem, but the flower's pink, there's a tiny wasp in it. I haven't seen this plant for years. That's because I haven't looked.' His tone was urgent with the effort to remember. 'I used to look at things,' he said.

Tina propped herself up on an elbow. 'What's running up and down it?' she said.

'The ants. Big fellows with sort of jaws, hundreds of them – heavens, they do look dangerous. What do ants eat? Do you know, there must be thousands of flowers in this field. I've just counted a square metre, roughly speaking. There are fourteen species, and that doesn't include the grasses. They're more interesting than the flowers when you look at them properly.'

He blinked, refocused, stared. An inch or two away a damselfly from the stream trod air, and in astonishment he jammed his glasses back into place to examine it. By then it had whizzed backward, pausing, a brief streak of sapphire on the immediate horizon, then gone. Kestner rubbed his eyes under the spectacles.

'I don't really want to die just yet,' he said, as if making a discovery. 'I need time to remember what all these things are, to find out. And why they're doing it.' He concentrated. 'Why are they doing it, Tina? For more than thirty years I haven't bothered to ask. I did when I was down here, you know, in the Army. Of course I had time then. I suppose time runs out when you take on responsibilities. I could look at this for ever, all these tiny questions running about, and they probably have no answers, but the scientific ones would be enough, wouldn't they? They're all in books. You can look it up when you get home. Explanations. Oh, well, maybe I'm wrong to expect them. But I'd like to know. A bit late, isn't it?'

'If you'd allow me to speak . . . ?'

Kestner took off his glasses and sat up; the putative biologist turned into a fattish man a bit tousled and blinking as if blind. He looked sheepishly himself again.

'I'm not paying you now to listen,' he said, 'so you might as well talk and then I can get my money back.'

'You're not going to die just yet, father,' Tina said.

Throwing back his head, Kestner grimaced upward at the sky, still permanently blue. He slapped the flat of his hand on the grass. Midges flurried up against the sun in riot. He seemed in ludicrous agony. Searching for a gesture to prove, once and for all, the point that he was indeed dying, he picked up his bottle of wine, still half full, and flung it in a sloppy parabola as far as his throw would carry it. Red wine gurgled in spasms off the air and the bottle crashed on stone in the gully where the rivulet ran.

'Tina, I am dying,' he said, teeth clenched as pity lifted into his throat. 'That fool Rydbeck, who delivered you and got rid of your measles or whatever and used to smoke all my cigarettes when we played backgammon, has given me a month, perhaps two. I won't see the summer out.'

'You thought I knew without your telling me?'

'Yes, yes,' Kestner shouted with an awful hilarity.

'You were right,' Tina said, also raising her voice. 'That's why we're here, isn't it? Let's enjoy it. You'll make a botanist yet, father, if you keep at it. Have a cigarette.'

Kestner lit up. He breathed out. The blue smoke pursued a lazy course into the blue and vanished.

'It's the best yet,' he said, grinning.

With an inward shudder Tina saw a fly settle on his hand.

Loaded with the detritus of lunch, they walked back to the car. The interior was hot. How much – money, property, insurances – had he accumulated in the course of his working life? Would all or none of it come at once to her and Henri, whom she didn't even love? She would spend it, savagely, oh, how she would spend it!

'In half an hour,' Kestner said genially, 'you'll see what kind of father you have.'

At the entry to the town the authorities had left up the pre-war sign, Lascaud-sur-Marn, the blue enamel now pocked with rust. To the same post they had attached two oblongs of similar size, the top one in French. *Souviens-toi*, it said. Below it the message was in English: Remember. There was nothing in German.

Three other cars were parked outside the gate, all bearing French numberplates. The Renault 18 was from Paris and had a baby-chair secured to the back seat. There was a Peugeot convertible registered in the Somme. The 2CV from the Pas de Calais was stuffed to the canvas roof with disorderly baggage. None of the owners was anywhere to be seen.

For some reason Kestner, who had spoken not a word for several kilometres, parked a little distance away from these vehicles. As they entered the long grassy street leading to the interior of the town, Tina felt her hand briefly taken, squeezed and dropped, rather like a farewell. From nowhere she registered a strong desire not to follow the rusty overhead wires of a tramline looping towards houses that seemed to have no roofs. 'Oh, look,' she said and walked away from her father to a wooden booth where a vague elderly woman with glasses sat hunched behind a display of guide-books and postcards. Kestner stood alone in the sun, staring at the rails embedded in moss, waiting.

Many of the postcards had been taken before the war. They showed vanished sunlight. Deep shadows cut a pattern of rooftops and chimneys along cobbled streets where one or two motor-cars of veteran design were stationed far apart. Shutters were open to the day. An uncertain woman clothed in black stood posing for the camera beside a well from which she had just drawn water. A group of residents was taking the sun outside a shop doorway, the women upright in pinafores, the men in baggy trousers lounging on the pavement, an urchin or two. There was the church embowered in trees, the short spire rising above the tumble of tiled roofs with deep eaves shadowing their haylofts. All was at peace.

But then in the same rack were photographs of superior quality, showing similar views of the town in ruins. The spire of the church had gone. Piles of rubble interrupted the pavement outside the gaping doorways of shops that had lost their signboards. Here and there a shutter hung loose on a hinge. There was nothing to indicate what human event or act of God had devastated the town and emptied it of those dimly contented and softly focused days before the war.

Tina turned to the guide-books. There were three, all in French. The cover of one bore the vicious red silhouette of a bird of prey as if painted in blood, beak hooked, claws clenched, with the name of the town blackly superimposed in gothic script. The second, aiming at even more sensational effect, carried the stark image of a storm-trooper, fully armed, helmeted, hatred in the eye, jackboots astride the smoking remains of what was recognisably this town. The third booklet, devoid of all such artwork, looked almost academic by comparison. The sober typography announced it to be the official guide, written by no less public a figure than Xavier Lorion, Mayor of Lascaud-sur-Marn since 1960, socialist deputy, author of a bestselling philosophical history of the Second World War, and currently holder of some fairly impressive office in the Government. Even Tina, who took little interest in the politics of her husband's homeland, knew the name of Lorion.

Without a word, not daring to trust her accent, Tina bought this volume. Not wishing to open it – a white band eulogising Xavier Lorion's civic dignity deterred her from a nervous flip through its pages – she nodded thanks to the old woman, who made no reciprocal gesture, and rejoined her father standing alone in the sun, flies buzzing unnoticed round his head.

'What happened?' she said in a whisper.

'Do you still not know?'

'It takes me time to read books.'

'Let us go and find out,' Kestner said.

Their voices, though low, carried in the silence. The afternoon was sultry, Tina's awareness of the weather suddenly strong. Perhaps thunder threatened. There was a peculiar stillness in the sunlight, a weight in the air that had already reduced Kestner to a sweat soaking his shirt and dripping off his forehead, and it was this wetness that had drawn the busy geometry of flies to his body. Yet he removed neither jacket nor tie. He walked, the flies keeping pace with him, at a dignified stroll, eyes front, at a few beats less than the speed of a dead march, until they had passed the shells of the outer houses of the town. Then he stopped, and turning with the faint knowing smile of a guide waited for Tina to catch him up.

'Here,' he said in hushed tones as if drawing attention to an architectural gem, 'is the Post Office.'

The telegraph wires were still there, hanging loose from their china knobs attached by rusted brackets to the edge of the roof, and the impersonal mouth of the letter-box gaped at chest level in the crumbling wall. But inside there was nothing, though a fascia board in faded blue mosaic still picked out some of the letters of the town's name. Bare floors, interior walls stripped and honed by years of weather, a blank: not even a memory, only the outline of one; to Tina, looking closely over the sill into its few sketched rooms, it all seemed further away, in time, seemingly in space too, than any place she had ever seen.

'It's funny,' Kestner murmured in the same impersonal way. 'That Saturday morning in June 1944 I wrote a postcard to your mother.'

'I didn't know you knew her then.'

'I had promised,' he said, pleased to confess a matter so honourable, 'that if I came back from the war we would be married. I had therefore naturally been sending her postcards. No one ever knew in those days whether they would get through. Perhaps I didn't want her to receive this particular one. I could after all, have sent it through my unit in Celles, couldn't I? But that morning, in the dawn, coming away from a short night when Bernard was expected back at any moment and we had made love over a bottle of champagne which I had managed to buy – oh, what it cost me – I posted the card in that box.' He looked at the gaping hole bemusedly. 'I had made up my mind, you see.'

'To do what?'

'Not to marry your mother – and perhaps not to survive.'

'But you survived.'

'Sometimes it's very hard to die,' Kestner said reasonably.

'Even in war. In any case I did marry your mother. She never received the postcard, you see. Because that Saturday afternoon an event took place in this town which rendered the collection of mail from that box a matter of trifling importance.'

'The fire?'

Obstinately, against the accumulation of evidence, Tina still tried to stick to some simple explanation for the disaster, in an unconscious fight against not only complexity but horror. Surely, error being all too human, the whole thing had been a mistake.

Kestner, however, was firm, though quiet. 'No,' he said, 'there was more to it than that. Most people can escape a fire. Here no one escaped. The fire happened only when they were dead.'

And at that moment Tina recognised the curve of the street where on the postcard that family had been grouped in contentment at the door of their shop, in modest prosperity, even humour. Her eyes told her that the pavement was overgrown with knotty tufts of grass. The shop was hollow, the accommodation above it open to the sky. Tina halted, an inkling of terror at last creeping over her skin. It had taken this physical instant, this plain fact of here and now against that soft image of pre-war reality, to topple her resistance: those people, yes, had died all at once. She swallowed this fact. In the same breath came the shock that her father, here beside her, who had by his own confession rejected the woman who had later given her birth, had taken a hand in the slaughter of that June afternoon. And for a few seconds her voice failed.

Bolted to the wall of the vacant shop, letters chiselled into the stone, was a square plaque announcing the number of male residents of Lascaud-sur-Marn who had been massacred on that spot where men had lounged for centuries. They had finished their day's work in the fields or in bakeries and garages or over there at the school opposite and in insurance or legal offices above the shops, tossing between them the small change of local affairs, passing on to their children the traditions of gossip as well as the sense of belonging. Ninety-seven was the figure killed here. And Tina's voice kept starting, then stopping.

From that moment, when Tina's mind still failed quite to click into the secret which Kestner had been striving with all his will, and against it, to tell her all along, neither father nor daughter found that they could speak. He was dumb for his own reasons. Her voice felt trapped in her throat. Thereafter, for the length of the afternoon, which appeared increasingly to stew in heat without breaking into any downpour, Tina felt her way into the continuation of the story. She dreaded its conclusion. Yet her eyes added one detail after another to a narrative which Kestner no longer had the ability to recount. It was beyond telling. For he had been here in 1944; and here he was still, her lifetime later. And nobody who had been here when he first came was alive to tell any tale at all. So his quietude became him.

They stuck together, of course. They drifted in the silence of tourists in any place of piety, whether an art-gallery or a cathedral or a tomb, she with a guide-book clamped under her arm, he detachedly not quite looking at wrecks and ghosts of scenes which he had known well. Back gardens, their very demarcations pathetic, the roses unpruned, were the nocturnal defences behind which he had slipped in and out of the town to visit his mistress. At the sound of local voices he had pressed his body into doorways that were no longer there. Behind upstairs windows that had no rooms inside them he had suppressed the cries of his passion. He had used the town as his unknowing pimp; it had hidden and protected and tempted him, by its normality, by its assumption that life would go on much the same, for ever, unless a husband like a music-hall joke came storming home at the wrong moment or an inveterate busy-body, perhaps that woman who stood by the well ogling the camera, told on him. These were the risks.

Tina did not know, Kestner couldn't tell her – but perhaps on second thoughts she knew – that on the night before the massacre the champagne which he had bought at so high a price, from a quartermaster who knew how often he slipped away from barracks, had been poured, and mostly wasted as its cork exploded in a dash of bubbles across the bed, to celebrate their ghastly choice: to take the final risk, to run away together, he to desert, she to abandon her Bernard, to go into hiding, across mountains, in woodland, on their slow way to the Mediterranean where one day, when perhaps the war was over, they would find a boat to steal or some fisherman to bribe into ferrying them wherever they wanted to go. That was why Kestner had posted the card, that dawn, to the woman he would later marry. He had been a bit drunk on no sleep.

Whether Kestner was recalling it or not, Tina caught none of this detail. It didn't matter. She knew. They came out into the Champ de Foire, a triangular space lined with homes which that afternoon had been abruptly voided. For Tina the statistics of disaster – how many German soldiers, how many French civilians – were without importance. She had only to look at the hollows of the hotel to know that families were at lunch in it, some perhaps under parasols outside, one or two having reached the coffee, others still poring with due weight over the menu, when all of a sudden whistles screeched, lorries swung at speed into the square, debouching soldiers who with a spurious respect herded everyone into the open space to await further instructions.

Tina plainly knew that this had happened. The plaques, here and there, numbering the male dead, quoting the date, told her. They unfolded in her imagination. Nothing her father said, and he said nothing, could alter it: she knew. So sure was she of these facts in that afternoon heat that for a moment she had the illusion that she could stop them happening. She believed that she herself had been present at this crucial moment, as she was now, and could either let it occur, and die with the rest of them, or turn back history into the good sense of leaving every detail just as it was: gossip at corners, savoury meals served at the hotel, the sun shining interminably as it did in photographs, her father falling so deeply into an enemy's bed that her mother would, after the usual delays imposed by war, receive the fatal postcard, mourn for a while, recover, marry someone else, have any number of children, live and die happy. And thus Tina would never have drawn breath.

The murders would not have taken place. But nor would she. She saw her father stand in bland perplexity in the middle of the square, blinking as if he needed his glasses, looking round at a ruined place in which, when intact, he had been unable to appear openly, except at the last moment when his bullets obeyed orders. And at that instant she wanted very much not to have existed.

A family of French people, perhaps mute refugees from the 2CV with all that luggage, wandered into the square. The only human sound among them came from an infant; maybe they belonged to the Renault 18 with the baby-seat from Paris. They strolled apart, awkwardly, now and then shushing the baby which threw back its head and screamed at the sun, then inhaled cunningly, dismissing the ruins with a podgy glance of ignorance, toothlessly gaping for a second before hurling its head against its mother's breast in a further tantrum. 'I know how you feel,' Tina muttered at it with an attempt at humour. Kestner was too far away to hear her. The family faded off to gloat vaguely over yet another macabre memorial, perhaps the well in the muddy bottom of which bodies were found, or the church, yes, the church. What had happened in the church?

Was Kestner saving the church till last? Why, why, why? He had dithered a very long time in the square. Obviously he had shot down a lot of the male inhabitants under their plaques, then set fire to their perhaps still alive bodies. Was it their bodies, those baggy trousers aflame, that had ignited the town? Tina's mind became suddenly preoccupied with the technique of doing so much damage. How did you accomplish such a catastrophe? But there was no doubt that Jannie had perished. Otherwise she, Tina, wouldn't be alive, would she? But how had she died?

Almost following in the footsteps of the French family, the

baby's protests still unconsolable, Kestner led the way, as if in procession, to the church. A young couple, whose careless clothes suggested the Peugeot convertible, was standing in the nave, eyes rolled up in a semblance of ecstasy to the smudges of burn in the roof. The girl, broad-hipped, wore a long dark skirt. Her hair was loose. But from her back view, as if deciphering code, Tina became aware, prompted by a sudden intensity in her father's presence behind her, that the loved one – what was her name? – Jannie had ended up here, yes, after the men were disposed of, here in this church where the women had sought refuge, no doubt under orders or at the prod of a rifle. And the children along with the women.

The mother's hand was patting the baby's back to no avail. It screamed on. Respecting the solemnity of a shrine, the rest of the family ignored it. Yet at once Tina thought that only the infant, but maybe also that girl who kept swivelling her face to her young man whose eyes were elsewhere, understood, or reacted to without let, the enormity of what had happened under the false hopes of the giant cross that still stood over the altar. She was guessing, of course. Or was her father, still amazingly casual, projecting into her mind information that was both accurate and beyond belief?

The church emptied. The baby's cry receded into the outer heat of the afternoon. The girl put her hand briefly round the man's shoulder and they drifted off befuddled. The church was left alone. Every detail of all this touched Tina as if she were seeing the last of the small, usually unnoticed gestures that made up so much of life. The vacancy of the church, or perhaps the concentration of its presences, made her shiver, and at that moment Kestner whispered, 'Yes,' sat heavily down on a knee-high tomb, slumped, put his head in his hands, and said, 'Come to me. I have tried not to have to tell you. I've been leaving it to you, hoping you would guess, and that would be enough. But it isn't. I must tell you.'

'Can't it wait?' Tina said, not wanting to come near him. 'This isn't quite the place . . .'

'This is the only place,' Kestner said, raising his eyes to puzzle at the church around him. 'Sit down, Tina. It won't take long if nobody comes. I've said it over so often before, but never to anyone but me. I always thought that starting it from the beginning was yet another chance of stopping the end happening.'

'Oh, *yes*,' Tina said, having thought the same.

Putting his hands on his knees, Kestner looked pleasantly across the spaces of the bare stone floors. His eyes saw nothing; that was evident. The events were taking place so inwardly that he appeared to be facing up to them for the first time, even inventing them, giving them the opportunity to surprise or overwhelm him. In his gaze, as the story developed, lay an ingenuous hope that at the last minute, when things became too much, he could personally step into the action as a redeeming hero and by lying, by editing, by taking control, divert the truth from the unspeakable conclusion to the tale. So often, at home, in the tram, chopping up meat, lying in bed next to a wife, he had done just that: permitted fantasy, in the nick of time, to keep him sane, to give him the hope of a tolerable tomorrow. But now it was too late for backing away.

'When I cycled back to barracks that Saturday morning after the champagne and posting the card,' he said, 'we were at once called on parade. That was unusual enough to start the rumours. The officers who had been with us ever since we came to Celles three months earlier, were jittery and told us nothing. We assumed they had sealed orders. The popular theory was – it wasn't any too popular in fact, especially with me, I can tell you, because that night was when Jannie and I were due to make our run for it – anyway, the theory was that we were going to be thrown into the battle up in Normandy. The invasion from England was about a week old and the bulletins said the Americans were only just hanging on to the beaches against brave opposition from our boys – who, I need hardly add, were said to be heavily outnumbered. So we, nice and fresh, were going to rush up there in lorries, singing lustily, and push the enemy back into the sea.' He raised his eyebrows as if surprised. 'But it wasn't that at all.'

'So you came back here?'

Kestner seemed not to listen. 'We spent most of the morning drilling with weapons and full kit. It was as hot as today. There was thunder around then too. It sounded like the war a long way off, and I was sick with worry. Not about the war. I was somehow never anxious about being shot or wounded – I'd never experienced pain, you see, it certainly wasn't courage. No, I just kept wondering, as the rumours went on gathering all morning, and the thunder threatened and went away, how I could escape to Jannie, desert there and then, advance our plans by a few hours – I even thought of getting to the telephone in platoon headquarters and inducing the Post Office at Lascaud to give her a message – madness! What could I have said? And as we marched endlessly back and forth sweating I could see my bicycle over there. It was leaning against a fence.'

He paused. 'I don't think I've ever felt so agonisingly alive or so close to not wanting to live – no, that's not true. But for a young man in love it had all the truth I needed. That bicycle. You can get so much truth inside you sometimes that it's almost impossible to breathe.'

Kestner took a deep breath. The church around and above him had vanished or did not yet exist. He was there on that parade-ground, the postcard of that morning still lying uncollected in the box at Lascaud, his mind alert to only one thought – Jannie, body and soul, an ache that consumed his brain just as terminally as the sweat punished his body under the weight of equipment: a pain that was balanced by one fear, the fear of making a mess of his escape, panicking himself into being exposed, humiliated, shot.

'In the end,' he began, then shrugged. 'In the end we broke for lunch – liver, high protein stuff to work up our energies for whatever was to happen next. I can't touch liver now, I never, do you know, never put it into my patés, well, perhaps chicken livers, people like them, and Jewish customers have come back to Lübeck, but never mind about that – and I left my place at table and slipped out of the hut, scraping the muck off my plate into a bin, saying I wanted to polish my boots but just to think things out, sitting on my bed. We still had no orders. And without even bothering to reflect – this is the odd thing – I marched straight over to my bicycle, as if under orders, and got on it and rode up to the gate and waved at the guards, who waved back, which gives you a clue to the sort of trust and informality we had in that camp – it was like peacetime except that it could only have happened in war – and started off on the road to Lascaud, knowing without question – this was quite insane, believe me – that I was doing the right thing.'

The church was very calm, only a fly buzzing in high zigzag under the vault. 'Think of it,' Kestner said. 'I even decided the world would be a better place as a result of the risks I was taking, all this sacrifice, my heroism. I imagined receiving a medal from the Führer himself after the war for preserving civilised values in the midst of conflict. But most of all, of course, I was drawn to Jannie as if she were myself. I longed to be where *I* was: in a field being told the slang name for a flower, in bed with my head nuzzling her flesh, eating food so hungrily that we couldn't stop laughing at our bad manners and so got hiccups and it was even funnier – all the things that were only memorable because we were in a high state of risk all the time, scared stiff.'

On the other side of the church stood a crushed pram next to a confessional and, looking at them, Tina began thinking that in a matter of seconds she would understand, yet all she understood was that both objects were self-conscious memorials to what she knew but had no wish to hear. Yet he continued, 'And so I cycled on – the journey usually took about an hour but never seemed more than a few minutes or less than a day, that's the contradictory way I thought of love – with my uniform on, my helmet, a pack of iron rations and odds and ends of underwear on my back, a rifle slung across my front, banging at intervals against the handlebars. I even had grenades on my belt, digging into me as my knees rose and fell and the lanes swished under the tyres. I know I thought it was such a wonderful afternoon. You smell things on a bicycle. And it was so funny the way the few French people I saw – a peasant stumbling along with a scythe, a pop-eyed old duck coming the other way on a bike – stared at me or wobbled and got out of the way, as though I were conducting a single-handed invasion of their country. Blitzkrieg – eh?'

And in the church Kestner chortled. Was he making a joke? Tina looked up at him. His face was suffused with – happiness? Or was it triumph? She had the sense that this moment on the lanes, racing southward towards freedom in his ridiculous outfit, had been, still was, the high point of his life. She had never before witnessed such a frantic poise in his looks: whatever had happened to him afterwards, for close to forty years, had failed that hour of rushing, against all the rules of decency, let alone the regulations of service, rushing towards the only thing he loved as much as himself, perhaps more than himself. With a lurch in her belly Tina realised that she had missed – sidestepping it at the moment of opportunity – any such experience. Meanwhile her father was chortling in a sacred place where hundreds of people had probably died, and here he was in his sixties enlivened by that disaster. But of course, by the odd standards he had established for his narrative, the disaster had yet to happen. He was still on the road, pedalling away.

'I had no second thoughts,' Kestner said, easing his buttocks on the tomb. 'I was just over half-way to Lascaud, within range of all the little spots we used to visit – did I tell you she never came without a gift? Goat's milk, smoked ham, everything tasted good then – when I heard behind me a rumble which I thought at first was the thunder coming back. The French countryside in those days was full of natural sounds, like the picnic we had just now.'

Tina tried to remember. That hour deep in the grass seemed years ago.

'But, you see, it grew louder. Then I thought, steering into the side, all those grasses brushing the spokes, it was Bernard – in the underground they always seemed to have petrol – coming back from one of his missions and making good speed to return to his faithful wife.' A frown crossed his face. He put thumb and finger to his eyes and rubbed them. 'It affected me then,' he said. 'It does now. Sometimes you can't conjure a laugh out of an irony, however long you live. In fact I knew that he would run me down. Nobody would know the truth of the accident. He would swerve on a blind corner, tip me headlong into the ditch, brake, come back, see the crushed bicycle, pick up a stone, ram it into my skull, and go on home to find Jannie reluctant to embrace him because she knew what was planned to happen that night. She might wonder where he had picked up a rifle. She would wonder more where I was. But all that rumbling behind me wasn't Bernard returning home.'

'Come on, what was it?'

He gazed at her loftily, as at a child, as if she had no right to ask questions. Then he said, 'First a motor-cyclist passed me. I knew him. Then a lorry. It was full of my companions. They gaped out of the back at me on my bicycle and the driver hooted. Then the second lorry cruised up behind me, trying to bump me on – obviously they were sharing some joke in the cab about my keenness – and the men waved their guns and started cheering. There was a third lorry too, bringing it up to about a hundred men in all – and after that came an open car with the officers in it. Some of the men shot out their arms in the old salute; we were fed up with it by then, most people preferred the traditional military one.'

To Tina's horror he sketched a version of each salute on the still air of the church. 'Never before had I achieved such popularity,' he said. 'I even grinned. I wobbled about like the old woman. And in fact it was eventually the staff-car which, honking away, pushed me into the verge. And the convoy stopped. For me! Everyone was in a high old state of excitement. They had got their orders, you see. The officers were far too relieved not to be going up to the front in Normandy to ask one another how I'd managed to become acquainted with the sealed orders before they opened their envelopes – and was now already on my courageous way, leading the entire unit with initiative and physical effort and devotion to duty!'

His voice, which reliving the episode had reached a note of triumph, now sank. 'I didn't know it,' he said, 'and you know that I didn't know it,' he added, 'but we had been ordered, by someone with no idea what he was doing – typical staff-officer stuff, I imagined – to come and punish Lascaud-sur-Marn.'

Tina drew in her breath. Knowing the rest in outline, she was nonetheless desperate to be told it in detail. It needed spelling out; her father, a dying man, required for his own sake to bequeath it to her. Never in her life had she sat somewhere, as on this tomb, where she so much detested herself for being. But there was no choice, even if it meant colluding with his guilt. Guilt? He was behaving as if he were at a party. The lads had tumbled him into the back of one of the lorries. They had thrown the bike in too, clapped him on the shoulder, shouted slogans and sung songs, almost as if the unit, after all the fuss and tension of the morning, had been detailed for an afternoon's outing in the country.

'You are told so little in war,' Kestner said, 'and that's wise of the authorities. It means they can count on instant obedience, even in acts which afterwards, when you have time to think, seem beyond the range of . . . I've had a long time to think,' he said with sudden violence.

Still no one entered the church. Tina ached for an interruption, if only because, stupid reason, that part of her which Henri had trained in Gallic notions of good taste revolted against her father's drone of German desecrating this inalienably French shrine. His pitch was low, but the words seemed not to disperse. They gathered under the blackened vault in guttural accumulations of language that recounted the unforgettable, they filled the spaces with the awful silence between the lines until her head thickened and she felt she must burst out into the air. But she stayed. She wanted nothing more than to block her ears to it. But as though joined to her father in more than kinship she had to stay to listen, just as crucially as he had to tell, with just as seemingly incestuous a drive.

'I couldn't believe what was happening, you know,' Kestner said. 'Amid all the singing and shouting, the speculation, the relief that we weren't going to war, I looked out over the tailboard of that lorry, the staff-car following us, the officers poring over maps, all four of them grave and pale and well turned-out, yes, elegant, and saw the countryside flowing past, growing more and more familiar to me with every second. A distant wood over to the right reminded me that you could probably still see, if you looked, the imprint of our two bodies in the bracken. Across that field, hidden by a steep bank where kingfishers had nested, we had dipped our feet in the shallows of the Marn, that's the local river. Here was a farmhouse where Jannie had asked for milk while I hid in their barn. My heart could hardly stand it, because I didn't know what it meant – it all seemed to be flowing away from me, even as our jolly band of comrades, being jolted about in the lorries and talking about our luck, got nearer and nearer the town. Up to the last minute I thought – as you think in a dream – that we would bypass it and go careering on south, and then, when we entered the main street and slowed down, I thought cunningly how I might slip away, while the officers were conducting some routine check, and find myself in Jannie's arms, quickly explain everything, and duck out of the back door with her and just run for it. But it wasn't like that.'

He stopped. The arrival had been timed for a quarter to two. By ten past three, eighty-five minutes later, nobody in the town was left alive. How did you bridge that space, how explain it, how use words to make it sound like sense? Nor had Kestner, he knew, left himself any means of skirting those eighty-five minutes. He had been there. He was there still. It had cost him these almost forty years to accommodate his mind to the almost greater extreme of bearing witness. Biting his lip, remembering the disease eating him, he set his brain resolutely back to a quarter to two.

'What we had to do was very easy,' he said, 'because nobody told us what it was until it was too late to avoid doing it. A man works by split-second timing, you see, if he has been well trained. We bundled out of the lorries in the Champ de Foire, with all the certitude of youth that believes in miracles. Why, the officers might be intending to treat us all to a drink, even a slap-up meal, in the hotel across the street where we could see people peaceably eating – the place had quite a reputation then, plenty of fresh vegetables and good meat, gourmets travelled from as far as Celles or St Rabier. But it wasn't refreshment we were being offered, because we were now formed up – this is when the joking stopped – on the square, while various locals going about their business ignored us, and detailed off into groups of three and told to round up everyone in the town, irrespective of age or sex, and bring them under guard here to the square, making sure that they had their papers, and be at all times polite – that was it, be polite. Who could be suspicious of an order like that?'

He paused. Tina said nothing. 'So we marched round the town, almost as if visiting, and courteously knocked on doors, and if old men started hiding in bedrooms we hustled them out, and we searched granges and back closets and cupboards and chided anyone trying to evade us, and looked at their papers, and herded them all off, in families, in couples, with their children – the babies made a bit of a fuss, I remember, but everyone else was very good, if a bit bewildered – yes, in about half an hour we got them all assembled and there was this great gathering in the square, where we thought our commanding officer, who was quite an impressive fellow, gift of the gab, good family and so on, was going to make one of those coldly civilised speeches I'd often heard, about not harbouring the Resistance and giving up the food they were growing, routine matters like that. And there was Jannie.'

He paused. Tina said nothing. 'I saw her at once. And, in a

while, she saw me. She was standing, hugging herself, next to a portly man who looked nice because he still had his napkin tucked into his collar from the restaurant and was thoroughly cross, but only because he hadn't been allowed to finish his lunch. Yes, she saw me – I'm almost sure. And she didn't blink or show a sign or bring out a red handkerchief or anything. She stood there with her arms folded, looking as if she knew far more than I've ever learnt. She knew what this was. She looked proud of it.'

'What was it?' said Tina tiredly.

Some French voices were murmuring outside the walls of the church. She strained to hear. Would they come in? They were discussing, argumentatively, the east window where someone had broken out: the only woman left alive; with her last strength she had clawed her way from the altar to the sill above, smashed the glass, then dropped to the street below and made off. Or had she? No, no one survived. The voices faded.

'It was quite simple,' Kestner said. 'We separated the men from the women and children. It seemed humane. But that was the worst for them, even worse than dying. We led the men off to their own barns, asked them to shift their carts into the open to make room, ordered them into corners – there was a smell of recent hay – and shot them. Yes, Tina, I fired that rifle which I had round my neck on the bicycle coming to rescue her. Then we set light to the hay, most of us had matches, I smoked cigarettes then, yes, just as much as I do now. Meanwhile the women and children came here. I do not know whether they were forced to come here. But they were in this church.'

He paused. Tina said nothing. 'I had by then killed a lot of men, Tina. It becomes a game. Once you start, you can't take it seriously, but you do. Cold blood becomes hot. You suspend yourself. It's like being in love. Nothing else, for the moment, matters. This appetite takes you over, and that bit of you which is doing it must, at all costs, complete the job. Or admit to failure. It's a clean break. You want everything to start again, with nothing there to interfere with it – it's the way revolutionaries think. I did not enjoy the thought of the bodies burning to cinders as the barns went up in smoke, but I knew that it had to be. Even if I hadn't been told the reason, whatever that was. And when we'd finished with the men, we gathered here, outside the church, just like those people now. And, do you know, the screams that came from inside sounded like worship, they sounded as holy as music – when voices go beyond despair, when people do, I . . . I didn't know. I still don't know. In any case I never saw her again.'

He spoke almost lightly, then threw a swift sidelong glance at his daughter, as if no longer speaking only to himself.

'That's not true,' Tina said.

Kestner smiled. 'I guessed you would know. I was testing you.'

'Nor is that true.'

'Not very.'

'There's no point in hiding the rest.'

'Do you really want to hear it?'

'No. You do.'

Almost in salute Kestner put out his hand. Tina removed hers. Then he said, 'All right, we were standing outside the church when the screams died down. Before they set fire to it – they were bringing up loads of hay on a lorry behind us – a detachment had exploded a canister of gas' – he pointed to the floor in the centre of the nave – 'just there. I don't know if it was thought to be a more humane way of seeing off the women and children, but I can only say that at the time it felt less unkind than lining them up to be shot. Then, as the silence grew from within, there was a crash of glass breaking round at the back of the church, though I could only just hear it because of the noise of the houses burning and the occasional rattle of shots from where they were finishing off the men. But an officer shouted and two or three of us were made to run round the outside of the building and see what was up. You can see the window from here.'

Again Kestner pointed, this time above the altar to a relatively small gothic window of plain glass set high in the bare wall.

'One woman had already jumped into the street from that window, and I saw the last of her running behind some sheds in someone's garden. As we came within view of the apse another woman clutching a baby had just dropped and was on her knees, and a girl was standing framed in the window, legs bent to leap, and yes, Tina, I would have known her anywhere. And then the officer again shouted a command behind us and we opened fire. I think I opened fire at least. I cannot be sure if I hit anyone and I don't believe she saw me.'

'Does it matter?' Tina said with a quick sob, tears starting.

'Yes, it does matter. It always will. It all matters. And the worst and last thing that I must say to you, as I have said it so often to myself, never really believing it, thinking I must have lost my memory, though I believe it now, is that at that moment the only feeling which the event aroused in me was one of relief. Intense relief. Look, Tina, I didn't have to risk myself any more. There was no evidence against me. I wouldn't have to desert from the Army. No longer would I need to shiver and shake with fear at the thought of Bernard suddenly coming upon us in his bed. All my love for her, which that night was supposed to carry me into lots of dangerous adventures of which I couldn't predict the end, was in a state of shock. I felt no love. That came later. I felt only this great pounding of relief all through my body, it was like feeling my heart beating again, beating normally, not half-way up my throat. I could even bear to look at her body, you know, lying somehow folded in half on the bank below that window, bits of glass scattered round it, the hair, which was dark with sweat, covering her face. Someone else moved it. It was burnt with a pile of others. I have relived those moments – it was now getting on for ten past three – so many times, but I have been unable to discover that I had any other emotions, except that through the shock of this escapade, this attack, my world had returned to normal – oh yes, and my throat was parched, and we were all dying for a glass of beer. I remember some corporal even saying it aloud and some of us cheering.'

'Let's go, we must go,' Tina said, her teeth chattering, the church was cold. Kestner walked slowly out into the heat, his limbs stiff, blinking at the light.

'I can't take any more,' Tina said.

A scent of roses hung in the air. The back gardens, which had been allowed to proliferate untidily through many seasons, were in full flower. The bird-song, which Kestner recalled as so touching a feature of the town, was at a low ebb. It was too hot for them, he supposed, and yet too early for the swifts which descended at evening. A family group, each member some distance apart from the others, was ambling ahead of them in wan respect up a ruined street; their backs betokened thought.

'Where's the car?' said Tina, fractious, her voice still hollow with tears.

'There's one more thing,' Kestner said, 'before I give myself up.'

Tina stopped, stamped her foot, setting up a puff of dust.

'I can't,' she said, regressing still further. 'I want to go home.'

'There's one more thing,' Kestner said obstinately.

'Look – those people,' cried Tina. 'I can't face them, they're French – don't you understand it? They're French, they're mourning, let's please go.'

Kestner walked gently on.

He had heard about the Museum, of course, from the literature that now and then arrived by post at his home in Lübeck, addressed to him under the false name of a supposed local patriot exiled in Germany for business reasons. Several times over Kestner read, with the aid of a dictionary, every book or pamphlet or memorial guide which the Conseil Municipal sent him, except the one Tina held, which was evidently new. He was aware of every detail of the way the mournful industry had grown.

They had built the Museum underground to avoid spoiling the ruins. It lay embedded in a series of concrete bunkers under a grassy esplanade close to the cemetery. With Tina still fretting behind, Kestner entered the cool chambers, which were laid out with the space and taste of a gallery of modern art: free-standing glass showcases softly illumined from within, rolls of honour framed on the walls, every item precisely labelled as though of outstanding aesthetic merit or archaeological value. Still a touch angered by Tina's childish hysterics – she was quite capable of understanding, if only she would calm down and be herself – he began to look critically at the exhibits, first passing his eyes over the endless lists of victims, whose names, ages and professions (if any) were recorded, to see whether there was anyone he recognised from the old days: that baker, for example, who was hard at work long before dawn in his premises opposite her bedroom or the lawyer whose brass plate glittering in the early light had cast a glow on the ceiling which faded in seconds as the sun rose higher. A sudden name might touch off a memory of an incident he had forgotten.

Yet it occurred to Kestner that perhaps the French were making too much of their tragedy. Forty years was a long time to pursue grief and to maintain in pious silence the asperity of such resentment. In the course of time, he thought, an element of vulgarity had crept into all their displays of unforgettable memory, even on memorials that stretched back to the Great War in which Kestner's father had been killed by them. Instead of pursuing the virtues of a fresh reaction to wars that were nobody's fault in particular, as he had, their addiction to old grief had become – what? Coarse-grained, not to say ill-mannered.

Kestner knew he had no right to these thoughts, as his eye wandered over caskets of misshapen wedding-rings torn off dead fingers and mashed watches stuck at any time from twelve minutes past two, when the first shots were fired, to half-past three, when the flames were already dying down – but he thought them. He could not deny that they were a part of him and so, with a logic that itself somehow excused them, these thoughts must come into the open, at least of his own mind.

And, again, another unacceptable thought, he still did not believe that he had been wholly in the wrong. His love excused him too. Yes, his love vindicated his actions by having made them so impossibly difficult to commit.

It was then, as he sensed Tina snivelling behind him, as he refused to pity his daughter for breaking down so weakly, that his glance fell upon a small, square, battered, silver object, tarnished, engraved with parallel lines that had been knocked out of true, lying by itself in one of the showcases. He identified what it was, turning cold for no apparent reason, a second or two before he recognised it.

It was a cigarette case, a small one, designed for a lady's handbag. It was bent and ruined because a small cylindrical object had struck it at an angle with great force. One corner was deeply scored by the passage of the bullet. The bullet must have passed on into flesh and bone for which the cigarette case had offered only partial protection. He looked at it long and hard and with a confusion of feeling, until he understood that he wanted the cigarette case, wanted to feel it in his hand, and put cigarettes in it for her, and then take it out of the breast pocket of the workman's blue she wore when they met at some rural point on the map, struggling and laughing over this sly attempt on his part to touch her nipple, and then in delayed reaction Kestner incredulously recognised it. He had bought it in Celles in a shop full of rings which soldiers less obedient to the official conventions of *politesse* simply stole from the old Jew for their girl friends, knowing he would never dare to report them.

But Kestner had paid for the cigarette case. He had paid with a delight that to his mind added much value to the present. He had filled it with the ten cigarettes which it accommodated without crushing and she had slipped it into the pocket above her heart, done up the button, with a sign that he would have to rape her, or so he understood it, if he wanted more than the strict ration she usually allowed him of his favoured drug. Scared of fire, the only risk she loathed, she never let him smoke in bed, except just that once, in the first dawn, when his young lungs expanded with a deeper pleasure than ever since. Whose bullet had hit the cigarette case? His?

Tina heard a loud dull bump. She looked up in shock from her bleary perusal of the list of names that went on and on: had he dropped dead? Her father was bent over a showcase, the glow reflecting upwards into his face, so that she saw his jowls outlined and the gross flesh of his cheeks pendulous in shadow, and he was rubbing the butt of his fist. Then he raised it to the height of a salute and again brought it banging down on the glass.

'Stop,' she said. She grabbed his arm. 'What on earth are you doing?'

Footsteps echoed down a subterranean corridor. They sounded official. Kestner's fist was still tightly clenched, his look furious. How could he digest the sight of the cigarette case, under glass, on display to any common eye that cared to brood on it? Only, it seemed, by regarding it as his property, an object on which he had spent money of his own, which he had every entitlement to claim and pocket and hide. Yet there it was, safe, painfully smug under the unbreakable glass, offering anyone who looked a sentimental release for their suspicions, fantasies, hatred. At that moment a trimly suited man with a depressed moustache entered the chamber and stared at them both as if they had profaned the proper silence. And feeling her father's energies sag, Tina gratefully led him away into the light.

They made their way, eyes narrowed against the sun, back to the car. Limp with fatigue, Kestner followed her without protest. He had no intention of sharing the story of the cigarette case with his daughter. It was too new, a fact he had never known, yet another opportunity to delay the further horror he had come here to commit: to place his person in the hands of the authorities at this last possible minute.

This new delay, engineered by Tina's interruption of his attack on the showcase, appeased him for a moment. He would certainly have been arrested if the glass had broken – or, if not, his offence against good taste would have involved him in

73

answering some hostile questions, not the right ones. His daughter had saved him from too easy a surrender. For years his thought that he might eventually act had been dogged by a fear, a reasonable fear to judge by the way the publications from France expressed their unbridled emotion, of being lynched or otherwise stilled, before he had a chance to make his points in public. They might have taken him into protective custody, but nobody would have listened to what he wanted to say.

They sat in the car. 'Let's please go back to Paris,' Tina said. The other cars had departed. The ruins were about to shut for the night.

'Not yet,' Kestner said.

'We could drive all evening and get home late, that wouldn't matter, La Coupole is open till two, we can have some dinner – Henri will be asleep, he always misses everything – and you'll be hungry by then, they have good beer.'

'Not yet,' Kestner said.

'You've done it now, you know, father,' Tina said, writhing against her head-rest in the heat of the stationary car. 'You've expiated it all. I understand the difference between love and hate – that's it, isn't it? Well, you've explained it to me. Do start, come on. We want to be on the road. It isn't far. There are lots of treats and chances and possibilities left, and I certainly don't mind, not any longer, that you've unloaded all this guilt on me. I'm your daughter. I shan't forget anything you've said or shown me today. I just want to get back to things as they really are, and you need that too.'

'Not yet,' Kestner said, starting the motor.

Across two fields watered by the Marn, separated from this ghetto of silence as the day at last cooled, stood the new town of Lascaud, rather larger than its forebear, hemmed in by small industries which had developed since the war. Much of the town occupied a slight rise which Kestner remembered to have been once covered by woods. He and Jannie had penetrated those glades two or three times until they discovered a small girl watching them make love. Nowhere was ever safe.

Now Kestner slowly drove into the town. It was an unappealing amalgam of high-rise housing divided by areas of worn grass, public buildings which looked like shut-down modernistic cinemas with vertical slits for windows, and plate-glass supermarkets inside which a few women wheeled overlit trolleys in slow motion. It was as formally planned as Richelieu, the town where they had stayed the night, but ugly, done on the cheap. On one corner of the main square, dominated by a town hall in grubby sandstone, massive but lacking all pomp, was placed a café littering the pavement with untenanted plastic chairs.

'How awful,' Tina said.

'Yes,' said Kestner. The whole town struck him as even more ironically arid a memorial to the deadly past than the ruins. 'But let's have a drink.'

'No, let's go.'

'Not yet,' said Kestner.

They entered the café. A dozen or so men lounged within, sharply divided into age-groups. A few, sitting glumly at cards, could have been alive when the massacre occurred. Like Kestner, they were somewhere in their sixties. If not from other places, perhaps drawn by the chance of work, how had they survived that day? They could have been away for the afternoon, visiting friends in a nearby village, off on Resistance duties while their families died. Perhaps Bernard himself was one of them.

To Tina's surprise Kestner asked her to order for him, in her less suspect French, a large draught beer and a brandy. She decided on orangina. The barman, who had a thin face, spuriously merry, was about her own age, born post-war. He grinned at her slyly, recognising a tourist; and tourists came to these parts for only one reason.

'Where are you from?' he asked.

'Paris,' Tina said shortly.

For the next ten minutes, eyeing his dumb contemporaries across the room, Kestner prepared his mind for the public act which he had so long planned. He said nothing of it to Tina. Instead he drank his beer, made her order another, sipped his brandy and thought, yes, he might manage a second, and talked in whispers, very much as if to himself, of his final encounter with Dr Rydbeck in the clinic at home.

His old acquaintance, companion of the gaming board, ruthless poacher of his cigarettes, had made few bones about his condition. While refusing to sully his tongue with any definite nonsense about cancer, he had given him – yes, given him, like a gift – at best three months before the pain or weakness drove him to bed.

'Meanwhile,' Rydbeck had said, 'I advise taking things easily. I have to advise that – professional duty. People sometimes take the advice, but then they lose what little they have left and spend all their time in front of television pretending not to worry. Go on smoking for heaven's sake. Drink yourself silly. To be frank with you, it won't make the slightest difference. In any case – you're a healthy man and still pretty young – it may not be the cigarettes at all.'

'What do you mean?' Kestner had said.

'I've no idea, not medically at least,' Rydbeck said in companionable tones. 'But people find all kinds of ways of killing themselves, you know. I've never studied you well enough to hazard a guess, but pointless anxiety – you know, a daily fear of nothing – sometimes eats into people, or they have a bad conscience for no good reason. Does that sort of notion ring any bell with you?'

'It might.'

'We both fought in the war, Ernst,' Rydbeck said. 'One can still die of wounds, even if one was lucky enough to escape the direct attentions of the enemy.'

'I know that.'

'There's much to be said for having only a little time left,'

76

Rydbeck said drily, half winking at his patient. 'My real advice is this, if you must know. Look into your conscience and decide whether there's anything on it. Look into your desires and determine which of them you haven't satisfied. And then take both off for the most perfect holiday of all, your last one. Don't forget to raise your glass in my general direction. Oh, I seem to have left my cigarettes somewhere – you don't happen by any chance to . . . ?'

In the café Kestner lit a cigarette, stood up, finished his brandy. He seemed about to launch into a speech. Then he stalked to the counter and to Tina's horror asked the bartender in German if he spoke German.

A silence fell. Two of the older men at cards skewed round in their chairs, aiming up the peaks of their caps at Kestner, as Tina hurried across the room and took her father's arm.

'What do you want?' she murmured in French.

'I want a simple answer to a simple question,' Kestner said. 'Who and where is the Mayor of this town? I wish to consult him on important business. Translate for me please.'

His manner was authoritative, his tone undeniable; the clipped syllables of his language, sounding almost like orders, hardened the silence. As requested, but tense with embarrassment, Tina translated exactly what he had asked, while trying to direct a shyly collusive smile at the barman. One man grunted, another uttered a derisive snort. The barman went on grinning at his regulars, while one of the lads lifted his nose from a sports page and sniggered loudly. Tina, who had hitherto been cursing her father's possibly drunken crudity of behaviour, felt, as the only woman present and deserving better of her husband's fellow-countrymen, affronted by this hilarious response to the old man's polite enough request.

'Why laugh?' she said sharply.

Still grinning, the barman shrugged and told her not to be upset. It was just that the Mayor happened these days to be a bit of a joke locally because this, his home town, was the one place in France which never saw him. His name was Monsieur

Lorion, Xavier, and he had shot so far up in the big world that he had left his old comrades far behind. One day he was cutting the tape at a chemicals plant on the Rhône. The next day they saw his picture in the papers escorting a lady not his wife to the Opéra. The fact was – everybody said it – that their old Xavier had become a snob, with an opinion of himself that had outgrown his modest days of fighting the Government single-handed to assert the rights of a farmer down on his luck or to house a poor family.

'They say he now thinks of putting his name up for the presidency,' the barman said. 'And though we're proud of it we find it hard not to laugh. He just ought to come and see us more often, sit here with the boys, stand us a glass or two. He's rich enough. Then we might enjoy supporting him.'

'Thank you, I understand,' Tina said gratefully, supposing she had glimpsed the rugged independence of French political thought. 'I shall tell my companion what you have said. He will like the joke.'

'No,' said the bartender. 'Just tell him to see the Mayor's secretary, Guy Bressac, he'll be over the road now, pretending to represent the community with a photograph of General de Gaulle at his back.'

'What's all this about?' Kestner said gruffly. Tina told him. 'Ah, good,' he said, strutting towards the door, aware that he must act soon as the minimal courage from the brandy would run out.

'Good luck!' someone called, and at this stroke of wit re-newed laughter shepherded the visitors into the square.

A tricolour flopped in a stir of evening breeze above the flight of wide marble steps that led to the portals of the Hôtel de Ville, which Lorion's construction company had built by public donation – another tribute to the massacre – in the early fifties. It was after five o'clock. Offices were emptying. A man on one crutch stood motionless in the foyer like a statue commemorating self-sacrifice. With fair grace Tina had given up struggling against her father's will. He was too near death to be worth thwarting, whatever the outrage to acceptable conduct he had in mind.

The veteran nodded with an attempt at sagacity over her request, made on her father's behalf, to interview Mr Bressac, vaguely sought reasons for refusing it by ranging his watery eyes over the vault, on which was painted in gaudy hues a montage of honest toil, then led the way up an only slightly less wide flight of marble steps to a door of immense height which no longer quite fitted its embrasure. Evidence of local craftsmanship, celebrated in the mural below, gaped near the hinges and it creaked when opened.

The bare saloon within, tiled with diagonal patterns that confused the eye, contained by way of furniture only two desks: one large, ornate, in the middle, unoccupied, clean of paperwork; the other small, in a corner, piled high with files, behind which sat a huddled man nosing busily into a ledger, his fingers closed tight over the nib of an old-fashioned pen. He allowed some spacious moments to elapse before looking up to acknowledge his guests. One of his grey anxious eyes was slightly out of true and his mouth was twisted from some accident, perhaps on a tractor; he had hayseeds on his sleeves. Tina momentarily wondered whether the very inhabitants of the town were not specially appointed memorials to conflicts of long ago.

'Mr Bressac?'

'It is rather late,' Bressac said snappily. 'But what can I do to help you?'

'I am a German,' Kestner said. 'I was here during the war.'

'In France,' Bressac said, 'we speak French.'

Unemotionally Tina translated her father's statement.

'Who are you?' said Bressac.

'I am his daughter.'

'You speak very good French.'

'I live in France because I am married to a Frenchman.'

'You are welcome, but I hope you have even better reasons for your sojourn among us.' Bressac chortled. 'You wish to buy a property in our region? There, I think, I can help. I myself own a farmhouse, only partly ruined, in an agreeable valley with views of unspoilt countryside. Or I might recommend two hectares of good grazing, within ten minutes by car of town, with its shopping, its smiling landscapes, its ruins of the past war, with permission already granted to build a modern residence thereon. Neither is expensive by current standards, but we can of course talk terms.'

'What's this?' Kestner said impatiently.

'He wants you to buy one of his properties and come and live here,' Tina said.

'Tell him that I'm only interested in making a statement to the Mayor.'

'Are you sure?'

'Shut up, Tina. Don't question me. Tell him. You're my only contact with them. You must please help.'

With a sigh Tina again translated.

'Statement?' Bressac said. 'What statement? I'm not a court of law. The police are available for this purpose.'

'He says he will talk only to the Mayor.'

'That cannot be arranged. The Mayor is a very busy man. There you may see his photograph, next to that of General de Gaulle. He has no time to listen to statements. What is this statement?'

She turned to Kestner. 'What do you want to say, father?'

Tina listened for several moments, while Bressac's mouth twisted in even more contorted annoyance. He plainly felt his time was being wasted.

Then Tina said, without expression: 'My father wishes to say that he was a German soldier in 1944 stationed in this region. He is ready to admit that he took part in the event during that year which made Lascaud famous throughout the civilised world. He believes that he has valuable evidence to put on record. With due respect he doubts whether he would be within his rights to say more except in the presence of the Mayor.'

'Why has he come here?' Bressac said irritably.

'I believe it is a matter of conscience.'

'It's too late. Far too late. This office is shutting within fifteen minutes.'

Bressac seemed unduly fussed, as if his mind lacked the resource to tackle this problem or simply failed to believe it. He gazed at Kestner with a shifty suspicion, as he might regard a criminal, not a criminal who had participated in a massacre of his kinsfolk, but one who by deceit or stupidity was reducing the dignity of a public official. As Kestner picked up from the man's expression unmistakable clues to the pettiness of his attitude, his determination to be heard, but only by someone of higher rank, hardened.

'Ask him if any of his relatives died at Lascaud,' Kestner said quietly.

Tina put the question.

'That is a personal matter,' Bressac said, turning a page of his ledger and sturdily making a pretence of concentrating on it. 'We all suffered here. Some of us were luckier than others. The Mayor himself, Mr Lorion, lost his mother, a sister and two grandparents. Nowadays – we are modern people – we prefer not to be reminded of it. We look to the future of this great town. Idle tourists – such as yourselves, with respect – are of no interest to us, unless they choose of their own free will to pay money suitable for whatever we have to offer them. You want a good restaurant? I will tell you where to go. Mention my name, and you will be accorded a princely welcome. We have a local fish, from the river Marn, which my brother – ask for Bressac, Jacques – cooks to perfection.'

During these words Tina, almost under her breath, had been attempting simultaneous translation, and from it Kestner was catching the edge of casual insult, not provably there but quite obvious, which had often been his lot, indeed that of all Germans, during his uniformed days in France. The back of his neck hotted up.

'Stop,' he shouted. 'For all I know I personally killed the Mayor's mother, and you have the effrontery to treat me in this scornful and unfriendly fashion.'

And Tina translated this too, by now once again, as in the bar when the men laughed, incredulously on her father's side.

Bressac stared at him, one eye hooded, the other tilting in shock, picked up the telephone and dialled a number.

'Come at once,' he said.

Within seconds, from elsewhere in the building, a cautious minion with a deeply down-turned mouth, wearing a suit of well-kept shabbiness, slipped into the room. His ears reddened as, at Bressac's request, Kestner repeated, and Tina translated, the secrets that had just been revealed.

There was a sepulchral pause.

'I didn't know that the Mayor's mother was dead,' said the newcomer slowly, 'so this man cannot be accused of murdering her, even if we knew that she was alive at the time of the catastrophe.'

'That's all hypothetical,' snapped the Secretary. 'The man is saying that in June 1944 he may have killed persons unnamed in this commune, and from the official point of view, if true, it is irrelevant who they were.'

'If that is so, and I'm not saying it is,' said the colleague in lumbering tones, 'then surely it is a matter for the police.'

'Then call the police,' said Bressac crossly; and as the man made to depart: 'Use my telephone.'

To Tina's ear these exchanges were not stupid. They struck her as a reasonably intelligent response to total perplexity. A man in his sixties speaking a foreign tongue did not customarily step into a municipal office inviting retribution for crimes that might or might not have been committed the better part of half a century ago in a country not his own. The underling, whose name was Domergue, dully and duly called the police station.

'We shall have to wait,' he said.

'Why?'

'There is no officer present of sufficient rank to conduct these investigations.'

'Let me speak to them.'

Bressac spoke with extreme rapidity – Tina understood

roughly that a wanted desperado was being held at bay in the Hôtel de Ville – then rang off with satisfaction.

'The police will arrive,' Bressac said.

Kestner understood. 'The police have nothing to do with this,' he said. 'I shall speak to no one except the Mayor.'

Tina translated. Domergue smiled thinly. Bressac planted his good eye on the photograph of General de Gaulle, allowed a yawn to twist his mouth into a cavern of assumed boredom, and waited. Within minutes a siren sounded briefly outside, then rubbery brakes. Boots were heard clacking unsubtly up the marble stairs.

Three policemen in uniform, one an officer, listened to the story in uniform silence. They turned their eyes coldly on Kestner; with no more warmth they swung their collective gaze back to Bressac, who was reciting a version near enough to the truth, as stated, to be beyond belief. Here was an elderly man admitting to a massacre for which the evidence had been somehow ennobled by the passage of time. The very fact of his drawing it to official attention after so long smacked of insult; it would have been in better taste to keep it quiet. Yet if a crime existed, in however delayed or heterodox a form the facts emerged, it deserved punishment; and yet again, if the suspect would submit his evidence only to the Mayor, who was in no circumstances available, no evidence could truly be said to exist.

The police said nothing.

Bressac turned to Tina with a lopsided shrug. 'Unless your father wishes to delay his departure – wisely, in my view – by accepting a meal at my brother's restaurant, and I shall arrange it by telephone, I suggest we forget everything that has happened between these walls and you return home, free to go about your lives as you wish, taking into account the fact that no possibility exists of his speaking to the Mayor.'

'Why not?' said the police officer.

Bressac glared.

'You know as well as I do,' Bressac said. 'I have Xavier's

confidence. He doesn't wish to be disturbed on trivial matters.'

'This is not trivial.'

'It is enough that it might be.'

'I submit that you should telephone him,' said the policeman.

Tina noted that the officer was at attention, too formally, as if mocking the laxity of civil authority. But her father was also at attention, oddly enough, feet together, arms by his sides, straining towards Bressac in a touchingly ingenuous effort to comprehend his every word, missing most of it, looking dull, then bewildered, a man already on trial for his life but misreading the messages. A chasm of pity abruptly gaped inside her. She had no idea that such feeling existed in her heart for her father's ridiculously honourable idiocy or such contempt for the lateness of its arrival. If only he had stepped forward earlier to confess all . . . but then she would not have been conceived. In which case she would never have had the chance of observing, with the irony he had taught her, this absurd battle of wills between men, elected to office, appointed by patronage, over whether to disturb a politician of whom they were frightened in whatever luxury he now happened to be enjoying.

'Telephone him,' said the officer.

'No,' Bressac said.

'Then we shall. I shall take it upon myself. France requires it.'

Bressac nervously waved a hand. 'My telephone is at your disposal.'

'Why are they talking about the telephone?' said Kestner.

'Even in France,' Tina said, 'protocol sometimes takes precedence over matters of life and death.'

Bressac looked up savagely. 'Here we speak French,' he said.

'In that case,' Tina said with spirit, 'you are unlikely to be accorded the privilege of hearing what my father has to say. Are you trying to suppress the truth? The Mayor will be most interested.'

Bressac smiled with barely courteous dislike. 'The Mayor will not be coming. I am in charge here.'

The officer had dialled. There was a pause, followed by so piercing a note in the instrument that he wrested it from his ear with a grimace. He then tried again, with the same result. Bressac abruptly stood up and snatched the telephone. 'On second thoughts,' he said tightly, 'I judge it preferable to speak to him myself, but you, sir, will receive all due credit for so compelling me.'

As predicted, the Mayor was not pleased. His voice gobbling inaudibly in the earpiece seemed to be making it clear that this interruption was as untimely and unforgivable as any other. 'You ask me, sir, for one good reason why this matter cannot wait,' Bressac said, unctuous with nerves. 'Allow me to put you in direct touch with the self-styled culprit.' And with a sigh he thrust the telephone at Kestner.

Kestner took it and uttered a greeting in German. In his ear a crisp brisk tone, rather deep-voiced, at once attractive, uttered an equally conventional greeting in the same tongue. With enormous relief, as if recognising at last the sound of a fellow creature, Kestner said, 'I wish to see you and you are the only person I am prepared to see. These men may not be fools, but their horizons are too small to give them any understanding of what I have to say, must say, and will say. On the Champ de Foire, in Lascaud, on 10 June 1944, I was one of a company of German soldiers who were ordered to kill many of your people. I am now dying myself. It is very important to me to make public the knowledge I have of that event, because I believe, since the news of my terminal illness, that I am in an ideal position to cast fresh light on it.' There was a slight pause. 'It isn't a question of wishing to pay any penalty,' Kestner added.

'Look, my friend,' Lorion said quickly. 'Say not another word. In particular, give no further information to those gentlemen about this or any other matter. They lack the experience to interpret it. I shall be with you in twenty minutes. Can you wait?'

'I have waited forty years.'

'Think carefully about that observation. It is a sentimental one, representing a weakness of thought, perhaps even self-pity, which is unlikely to improve our understanding when we meet. You understand?'

'Your tone of voice assures me that I do understand – and your German is excellent.'

'I learnt it to fight you,' Lorion said, ringing off.

'That also is sentimental,' said Kestner to the buzz in his ear. Then in French, at large: 'He comes.'

Twenty minutes passed. Kestner, as instructed, said not a word. Since no one had invited him to sit down, he stood, drooping slightly but with a very faint smile that betokened a modest pleasure in achieving his aim thus far. Bressac sat at his desk pretending to work, his eyes globular with affront. The policemen stood their ground, awaiting without hostility either dismissal or leave to arrest. It was the sight of Domergue against the wall, under the framed photograph of Xavier Lorion, lighting a cigarette, that reminded Kestner to his astonishment that he himself was not smoking. It was as though his nerves were anaesthetised by his own audacity. Then a roar of motor-bikes swept into the square and halted with a choke and a grumble, to introduce the purr of the limousine that followed them. Doors slammed. 'Two minutes,' Lorion's voice called, and within seconds he was in the room.

Without a flicker the Mayor stood just inside the door gazing at Kestner. They were roughly of an age. They would know without consultation what events had racked Europe in their lifetime. His confidence growing, Kestner met the slightly ferocious, selfish, wry glance of this contemporary, who was losing some hair and gaining some weight, who appeared to be compact of intelligence, if not intuition, certainly authority. A shortish man with sharp horizontal shoulders narrowing past his hips to disproportionately tiny feet, Lorion stood with his heels together, motionless, almost as if modelling a swish suit, one button smartly undone, the tie neat, a pin glittering, the shirt crisp from the laundry; but the strength was in his eyes, which were set wide apart and unblinking and very dark. An ugly nose, almost a boxer's overhung a mobile and thinly ironic mouth, now firm, giving little away: the tense pocked face of a man of affairs who needed to know it all, and would listen to it, then judge it, before himself making a single move. Kestner simply stared back at him, without fear, as if into a mirror.

'Nothing that has been spoken in this room – that general rule, often ignored, must be applied with rigour – will on any account be mentioned outside it,' Lorion said without raising his voice. 'The police, whose presence is unnecessary, will now leave and make no report.'

He was still gazing in cool fascination at Kestner. The police departed.

'You, Domergue, will return home to your charming wife as if nothing had happened, for the obvious reason that nothing has.'

Shoes tapped obediently over the tiles. The door closed behind the minor functionary.

'I am pleased, Bressac, that you had the courage to telephone me,' Lorion said, rewarding him with a brief glance, 'but I shall be displeased if by tomorrow I learn that the cafés are astir with news. While I have no power to deter people from spreading information indiscriminately, I can at least ensure that they later regret it.'

Bressac stood, screwed his pen into its cap, closed the ledger, placed it on a shelf behind him, glanced at a sheet of paper, dismissed it, ensured that the telephone was in position on its holder, locked the front drawer of his desk, checked that the pen was in his pocket, looked back to make certain the ledger was upright, folded the sheet of paper, slipped it under his blotter, gave Xavier Lorion a look of unplumbable hatred combined with both worship and regret, as if love and trust had been finally betrayed, and left the building without a word.

There was a pleasant silence.

'This is your daughter, I see the resemblance,' Lorion said. 'She is very good-looking and my wife will enjoy her company.

You will both be my guests tonight. I am not usually quite so arrogant, dictator though some consider me, but I feel that the circumstances warrant it. In other words, I prefer to keep you – within range. You will find my home agreeable. If you have a car, as I assume, I suggest you leave it here, taking what overnight baggage you require, and accompany me in mine. I do not prejudge the nature of whatever you may tell me, but I know that witnesses often succumb to a nocturnal desire to run away from the truth, especially after telling it. You will, however, be among friends. Even my enemies would grant me that. Is this plan to your liking?'

'Yes,' Kestner said, taking Tina by the arm, Tina returning the pressure with a shiver.

And Lorion led the way.

In luxury they drove for twenty minutes down a series of straight but narrowish roads. The outriders ahead set a high speed, waving into the verge a string of cyclists, family cars in rapid succession, a tractor pulling a load of hay. The sun was in their eyes.

The escort peeled off at their approach to tall white gates which opened as they slowed down. The guard, in police uniform, saluted. In front of them, across a stretch of unkempt parkland where wild flowers were shedding petals in an evening frisson of breeze, stood a grand decrepit survival from classical France, the pillars of the portico rising to a chipped pediment, a patchy frontage of tall windows vanishing into the shadow of taller trees. The drive curved past a stable-yard where a horse pawed the cobbles under a stopped clock. It looked forbiddingly peaceful.

'At this stage,' Lorion said, 'I often launch into my tedious history of the house – it's called Auzances – but I'll leave the honours to Marie-Louise. I'm very proud of it. Proud most of all of my acumen in accumulating the fortune to buy it. That, of course, took place conveniently before political reality led me into becoming a socialist. And I'm proud of that too.' He smiled. The car drew up on gravel. 'Now you know me well,' he said lightly.

Looking both eager and vulnerable, Marie-Louise Lorion was standing in welcome at the ornate doorway. Tina carried her small suitcase up the steps.

'Let me take that,' said Madame Lorion. She had greyish hair knotted untidily, a slim body, but large-breasted, big-hipped. Her mouth wore an uncertain lopsided smile.

'My name is Tina Boyer,' Tina said, as they trotted up a generous staircase. A drawing as sketchy as a Matisse caught her eye, a single line that became a plump woman in pencil. 'You don't know me . . .'

'Oh, I know you well enough to suggest a hot bath. Then a drink on the terrace? Open your shutters – but beware of mosquitoes – and you'll know where we are. Listen for the chink of ice. It always gives us away. Xavier calls it an aural oasis in this desert of a house. Come down when you're ready.'

Putting the suitcase on the bed, Madame Lorion left Tina to drift, incredulous, hands clenched tight. The room was high and wide. It had mouldings of wit overhead, a cherub, an angel. The pictures on the walls were so familiar as to be obviously reproductions. Yet Tina found to her shock that she was scraping off the paint with her thumbnail. A sumptuous bed bounced her body up and down. From the window, where mosquitoes hung, a view filled the room like a landscape: not too dramatic, just a surround of well-placed trees in the distance, enclosing a meadow ambered by the sun, in which horses grazed up to their knees, as hazy as creatures in a myth. On the bedside table a disordered pile of books smelt faded and brainy; some still needed the pages cutting. Tina's memories of the day dissolved into a hot bath. As the steam rose she heard muted voices from the terrace, where pots of annuals were positioned at vivid intervals. She stopped thinking, eyes half closed. It was a miracle.

Down below, after returning a backlog of calls from Paris, Marseilles, Paris again, then London, Lorion found his wife in the kitchen. Against his instructions – they had servants – she was filling a bucket with ice.

'Why are you doing that?'

'Who are they?' she said.

'She is a nice woman currently in shock,' Lorion said. 'She has just learnt that her father took part in the massacre at Lascaud. He wants to rub all our noses in it because he's dying. This would be a mistake.'

'What an awful childhood she must have had. Poor thing.' She dug a bottle of champagne into the ice-bucket and turned it once or twice.

'Childhood's a risk we all take,' Lorion said.

'Is that an epigram in your book?'

'Not yet.'

'Well, here they are,' Marie-Louise said, pouring almonds from a jar into a bowl. 'Are you as usual regarding an unexpected event as a potential crisis?'

'I mistrust the face value of everything.'

She wristed the champagne once more, then took a further pair of bottles from a fridge with wooden doors. A puff of icy mist came out. It started keening. She said, 'Is it because of . . . ?'

Very quickly Lorion said, 'A candidate for higher office cannot afford the riot of publicity which would surely break if his name were to be associated with the sudden emergence of a self-confessed war criminal, because the alchemy of the press is such that those sections of it hostile to his ambitions would ensure that some part of the guilt adhered to him and his reputation.'

'Oh, well,' said Marie-Louise.

'That is not all.'

'I never supposed it was.'

'I don't need time to think,' Lorion said. 'I know what I think. I need to know how I feel.'

Opening a bag of oiled paper, Marie-Louise poured black olives into a dish. 'You're still involved?'

'In what?'

'You know quite well.'

'In Lascaud? Yes. Only because I wasn't there.'

'Thank God,' said Marie-Louise.

'Why?'

'Otherwise you'd be dead. You wouldn't be able to hate me for preparing drinks for your guests.' She smiled. 'Look, it wasn't your fault that you were miles away at the time planning to kill lots of Germans.'

'That is not the problem.'

'What is?'

'I like the man,' Lorion said, picking a bottle out of the ice to open, scooping a few almonds into his mouth.

'Beware.'

'Of what?'

'One of your famous slips.'

Lorion bent swiftly, clamped the champagne between his knees, screwed the cork hard against the ball of his thumb, grinned as he felt it give. There was a muted pop. A few bubbles dribbled into the air.

'Perfect,' he said, still chewing nuts.

Lorion bore half a glass of champagne to his study and sat for a few minutes alone in the horizontal light. Far away he could hear the murmur of his guests gathering on the terrace. The room boxed him in books, the late sun fading along their backs.

His 'slips' were indeed famous.

More than once over the years he had unnerved his political staff by letting some quite unimportant slight pitch him into the irrational. No one had forgotten that evening with General de Gaulle in early 1968. At dinner the old boy, to gain some quite different point, had suggested that the good men of the Resistance, however brave, had been living off the fat of southern France, if only in a spiritual sense, while his army of liberation starved in the intolerant climate of Britain during long years of a waiting war.

At once Lorion had risen to his feet, upsetting with his napkin the presidential wine-glass, and coldly said, 'You are mistaken, sir. Not for the first time are you proving that arrogance is the child of power and our great past the victim of senile memory. In the name of truth and of the heroes of France, I ask you to withdraw those words.' The President, his white waistcoat bespattered with wine, allowed the moment to pass quietly into history by leaving the room, but a week later a number of personal letters from the Elysée arrived in the homes of notable families in and around Lascaud-sur-Marn, advising them that their representative, who had lost control of his tongue on a public occasion, was perhaps in need of a spell in the wilderness.

A few days later the President was rejected by referendum, thus confirming Lorion locally as a man of prescience. Legend soon spread the word that he had launched his attack only to remind De Gaulle that, like everyone else, he was subject to the implacable laws of human failure. Well, the incident had strengthened his power base. But Marie-Louise was right: his flashes of temper had the power to encompass his destruction.

Lorion sipped his champagne. Such mistakes bit into his friendships, now and then shadowed his marriage, had hurt his children, but the origins always lay in that June afternoon, in Lascaud, in his absence. When challenged by some affront or insensitivity, his mind did not formulate thought, but exploded into passion. By courting disaster for himself, as politician, husband, father or friend, he was still defending his family whom he had let down by being away, albeit fighting for them, when they died. In his outbursts, which were sombre celebrations of a continuing wake in the depth of his mind, he almost believed in his power to bring that vanished family back to life, if only he sacrificed his success, his future, his efforts to shape France into a country where no such event as the massacre could recur. He had never mastered his distaste for being alive at the expense of his mother, grandparents, a sister, whom he might have saved from a contemptuous death by shooting them, then killing himself. But he was elsewhere at the time.

Yes, he must beware. It still hurt. In the same moment Lorion finished both his drink and his thought. The sun was setting in a brown light on the paper spines of the walls of books. He stood up, put down his glass, paused. A telephone rang in another part of the house. From the terrace sounded murmurs of assembly, the chatter of ice into glasses, an undercurrent of the developing pleasure of an evening he would miss.

For now he must go and find and face the German.

'Aren't you Louis Larguier?' Tina said.

'That's my name.'

On the terrace a middle-aged man took Tina's hand and kissed it with gallantry. His delivery was slow, almost anxious, the words grizzled by his moustache, the eyes wicked. Tina felt silenced by his fame. He was staying with his old friend Xavier because tomorrow night he had to perform for charity in Lascaud. Did she know the place? She knew it. Not only had he and Xavier fought a war together long ago – she was far too young to recall such foolish antics – but together they had enjoyed many of the ups and downs of politics over the years. 'And what do you do?' he said in a languid growl. 'I'm a singer.'

'I know that. My husband loves you.'

'That is very flattering,' Larguier said, 'but you are the one he should love.'

'Oh, I love you as well.'

'Even more flattering, but you still haven't told me what you do. Never mind.' Tina detected the edge of tedium; his eyes were less merry. 'I must reluctantly give you up to these handsome young men,' he said, glancing with a disarming malice over the small groups assembled under the parasols. 'I believe William there is English. Aren't you from Germany? That would make a good traditional combination, wouldn't it? And I gather he lacks all principles, as the English do, which is a delightfully unfair advantage in matters of love.' And Larguier sweetly bowed, before drifting off to embrace his hostess.

The young men lacked much of the romantic emphasis with which Larguier's irony had burdened them. One was pompously rotund, a conservative careerist in his thirties, recently elected to the Chambre, his eyes bulging ambition which had the look of lust. He tried briefly to hector Tina into taking a stroll in the grounds with him, then gave up and talked irritably of international misunderstanding. Then there was a thin sandy fellow with a sanctimonious mouth. His line of seduction was to explain in limpid whispers how to design an opera without permitting the visual element to overwhelm the music. Tina had heard his name during one of Henri's periodic assaults on the heights of culture. An opera designer himself, he was obsessed with his credentials. As if training her, he began drumming into Tina the humourless rudiments of the craft.

Tina was unused to such company, even more to its egotism. But every minute struck her as a pleasure she had no right to expect. She felt the sun sinking on her face. She was sipping at leisure a champagne that was superb. Any of it was better than Henri's cocktail of bad temper, hangover, and complaint against the injustices of life.

Then, on her third glass, Marie-Louise Lorion introduced her to William, a journalist from London who was engaged in following Xavier's daily routines to write a book about his life and personality. A floppy head of hair bent awkwardly low to brush a kiss across Tina's knuckles, and she was looking up into a pair of thick spectacles and gaunt cheeks that had been shaved only patchily and hours ago. 'Enchanted,' he said with enthusiasm, slopping his drink on some petunias. 'Fair warning – I'm a reporter, so say nothing. Now what shall we talk about? I'm interested in women, which the psychologists attribute to a lack of more serious ambition. Are you interested in men?'

'Only if they happen also to be human beings,' Tina said.

'A nice point. A nice distinction, that. I must remember it. How could I not? It might prevent me in the nick of time from making passes at every woman I meet.'

'Do you do that?'

'Well, yes, but I'm not attractive enough to rate a very high average – I suppose that's the mark of a human being? We're fallible, we humans. I fail at almost everything, in fact. I know beauty when I see it, but that ends up in failure too, because I lack the charm to win it over. Should I change these glasses, do you think? I'm not good at personal hygiene either, you see. I can't see myself in mirrors if I take off my spectacles, and my hair's awful, don't you think? Not that I mind being me. That's fairly obvious, isn't it? Do you like honesty in your men?'

Tina laughed. None of it was either honest or funny, but anyone so consumed by the vain longing to be liked, by the force of being alive, melted her. Here he was, with some elegance, throwing out his problems for anyone at hand to solve. But what of hers? What of that afternoon's revelations? What about people reduced to bones and ashes, brains shrivelling, children gasping down that gas, which she had inherited today from her father? His bequest was also a gift of ego. It was better, or was it worse, to keep the balance, as her marriage did, and never to stray into the barbaric areas where the truth was. Then she said, 'I think I'll get on with you.'

'Oh, good – why?'

'You're selfish and you admit it.'

'Quite right,' William said, frowning briefly. 'A splendid point. It's nice to discover something in my favour. I'm quite myself again. Despite all these other hangers-on – successes, horribly full of themselves – I shall now do my best to get you into bed. Tonight. I certainly can't wait any longer. What did you say your name was? You really are awfully sweet.'

'And what did you say you were doing here?'

'Apart from seducing you? Oh, just writing a sort of book about Xavier.' William paused. The last of the sunset flashed on his glasses. Someone's ice rattled. Tina heard a mosquito close to her ear and just beyond it nightingales starting in the dusk of the shrubs. 'You see, I'm trying to get at the truth,' William said.

On the gravel beyond the house Kestner, escorted by his host, was ducking into the passenger seat of a Renault 5.

'We are dining alone together,' Lorion said, as he took the wheel and drove north-east towards Celles.

'That's generous of you,' said Kestner, his mood easing. He had not liked the confinement of his huge room. 'I am not used to high society.'

'Nor am I. I merely depend on it for my politics. During the war, whenever we could, we met at a restaurant in a back street in Celles, where your people never dared show up for fear of upsetting the balances of arrangement, Pétain's armistice. The place is still in business and quite unchanged. It was established before the war of '14–'18 in the style of that era and it is one of the few resorts I know where the past is respected. One waiter fought at Verdun. Another survived the destruction of the old quarter of Marseille when the Nazis flushed out our patriots by burning it down. I am very much at home there. It is secretive, because old-fashioned. In any case delicious.' Lorion paused. 'I hope it will refresh you after a day that cannot have been easy.'

'I had to tell my daughter.'

'She's in good hands,' Lorion said.

They drove on in silence through a deepening twilight.

The Salon Courtine, unannounced behind a terrace of crumbling Second Empire mansions now occupied by legions of the retired immured in small apartments, was approached through a courtyard heavy with the aroma of citrus trees in grand tubs. Lorion turned a gilded door-knob. Curtains flapped aside. The foyer revealed an aged dame on a high stool behind a cash-box chained to her wrist. By merely staring, through wrinkled eyes lustrous with cosmetics, she could see in an array of rusted mirrors on the walls the turn of events in either of two dining-rooms which stood at right angles to each other, repeating those repetitive events endlessly in reflections that were obscured only at the edges by swathes of brocade from which weighty tassels hung. Cut-glass chandeliers provided from on high a discreet illumination. A few couples sat at widely separated tables, their talk dimmed by the acoustics. The only loud sound, as slow as the beat of a pendulum, came from the clack of the soles of the feet of the waiters on the parquet, as they drew near over long distances from the kitchens.

No sign of recognition was offered Xavier Lorion as he unfolded his napkin. The policy of discretion had survived two wars. The whole establishment, which seemed on its last legs, was an honourable image of the old grandeur of provincial France, which Kestner had thought dead. He glimpsed suddenly at the back of his mind that expostulating visitor, turfed out into the Champ de Foire by the butt of a rifle, with the napkin still tucked under his double chin, to die.

Lorion seemed in no hurry. Ordering slowly from the inalterable menu, he recommended the *filets de sole*, poached in a sauce devised by old Courtine himself in the great days. It would not shame him now, he murmured. Kestner nodded to every suggestion: after the fish a wild duck to share, then perhaps a morsel of a local cheese. 'Thank you,' Kestner said gratefully, relieved of decision. Lorion's act of hospitality, taking over his life, freed him from responsibility, if not guilt.

They waited briefly for the bottle of St Pourçain to be served. 'It is undistinguished, but I drank it in childhood,' Lorion said. Each tasted the wine. Kestner sipped and pretended to savour, recognising the need for collusion. His stomach soured and gurgled up his throat, but he repressed the belch. Then each chewed some bread, Lorion tearing off little bits and tossing them into his mouth, Kestner pushing plenty of crust between his teeth, both gazing at the mirrored distances of each other across infinitely repeated rooms that lapped away into the past. Lorion had chosen his place well. Despite the elderly waiters who came and went, it was far from public. The body of the restaurant was as private as a memory.

'You asked to see me,' Lorion said. 'Here I am. Tell me what you wish.'

'I have already told the story once today.'

'Try it again. It will be different the second time. Not a

confession saved up for years, but a narrative owing its passion to detachment. You're another person now. Facts change their nature as readily as people can. There is nothing absolute about either.'

Kestner frowned over these words, but, detecting encouragement in their apparent logic, began his story, which for fear of boring his host now contained less material than he had vouchsafed to his daughter. He concentrated on the murderous outlines and on the possible excuses for his participation.

Meanwhile he unwittingly ate the nobly garnished fish. He said that he had enjoyed cycling in that countryside, exploring its secrets, as he strove, while in enforced exile from his homeland, to get spiritually in touch with the race and place which his superior officers had conquered. He mopped up sauce with bread. He did not know that, while listening at several levels, Lorion was summoning up, without pity, purely as fact, what little he remembered of his grandparents living out their docile senility in Lascaud, the slightly more he recalled of his mother who had always kept in the background of even her own life, and the essentials of his sister whose sexual laxity had always led her maddeningly astray.

Warming to the truth, Kestner then compensated for his excuses by admitting that he had fired his weapon at a woman unknown, but nursing a baby, who had leapt out of the church window in a blind effort to survive, but that up to that last moment, for which he had no wish to evade responsibility, he had been on the point of deserting the Army for personal reasons that had no bearing on his evidence. He drank wine without noticing its flavour. He did not know that Lorion's first thought was that this woman, any woman, might have been his mother or sister, the trouble being that after so long he could no longer rescue his emotions, as he had so intensely felt them at the time, from the moment of returning to his town from secret business to find the smoke still hazing off the wreckage of the barns, the church gutted, the bodies unrecognisably laid out on the makeshift stretchers of shutters or still piled at street corners, the enemy gone. Lorion's knife cut into the pale juicy duckling.

Kestner then described how he had set fire, as if in a dream, to those heaps of corpses and how the officers had demanded that the faces be unidentifiable, which to the lower ranks meant averting the eyes and hammering the dead to a pulp with a weapon, but that all this had not at the time seemed as cruel or mad as it must in this later account of it. He forked into his mouth some potato layered in cream. He did not know that Lorion was sensing that none of these facts, however hideous, was the whole truth and that he was doubting Kestner's ability to accommodate himself to the whole truth, whatever it was, before he died; and that the threat of death over the man was more likely to be a liar than a sense of life. Lorion then drank half a glass of good burgundy at a gulp.

He knew at least that his mind was working at top speed. He did not know that Kestner too had realised that he had conveyed so little of the story, edited this or that bit out, pressed one emphasis and lifted the weight from another, that he felt it was almost too late to confess: and proud of that. Only Tina would ever know the truth in full, and she lacked the experience to tell it as it was; history would never know. He laid down his knife and fork, deeply satisfied with his meal, noticing again with pleasurable surprise the wisdom of their setting, which took him back in atmosphere to long before he was old enough to commit any crime. With castors rumbling over the parquet a trolley of cheeses reached their table.

'Very well,' Lorion said. 'I may ask you questions later. For the time being I shall be quite frank in acquainting you with my view of the problem.'

'But the problem is entirely mine.'

'No,' Lorion said. 'We were the victims. We also have the right to confess.'

'Yes, but civilisation is utterly on your side.'

'Side? Why are we talking of sides? It isn't a competition. I don't seek to score off you. I don't think you realise what has happened to Europe, my friend. Let me tell you what I have managed to achieve in my short lifetime, largely thanks to what you helped to do that afternoon in Lascaud.'

A waiter with a knife hovered near.

'Ah, cheese,' Lorion said. 'Local cheese, goat's, that's the best. But you probably remember it.'

Kestner saw her fingers smeared with the damp of the cheese, offering it to him in the heat. The sunlight ran the length of her bare arm.

'I did eat them once,' he said.

'There's no time like the present,' Lorion said, drily emphasising the banality.

To Kestner's sadness the flavour on his tongue evoked no particular stab of memory. Also he had hoped more from association with this man's recollections, more of things he had perhaps forgotten. No such kick both to focus his life and to forgive it took place. Nothing happened. He waited while Lorion relished as ever the excellence of the cheese he had known for ever.

'I came back home to find what you had left,' Lorion said. 'The place was still alive, but only because the fires you started took days to die down. The corpses were so black as to have no human relevance. They inspired not feeling, not even rage – but determination. No question of revenge. Perhaps the few survivors felt it, perhaps the many outsiders did – the whole of France rising up in a lust for vengeance. But I didn't. I thought only that history had made one of those rare wonderful mistakes, so offensive to the hearts of our people that history could never be the same or as bad again.'

He sluiced wine over the last of the cheese on his tongue. 'Do you consider that intellectual?' he said. 'With me it's an emotion. I simply felt, with everything wiped out behind me, like the first man on earth. It wasn't even a matter of starting up again. I had to start from scratch. My father had died in 1938, from breathing in the dust from hay, a silly complaint but as fatal as any other. The rest of my family, which would have kept me quiet, by manipulating the conventions, by its need for love and normality, by its longing not to be shocked, were all busily alive – until you killed them, if I'm to believe you.'

Lorion stared. Kestner said nothing.

'So there I was alone,' Lorion murmured. 'In my home town on a summer's day. The circumstances were so brutal that the first thing I knew was that I mustn't fall into the trap of reconstructing the past. It hadn't worked. Here it was in ashes. You could no longer eat a civilised lunch and expect not to be shot and burnt. You could no longer make love to somebody without being dragged into the street with your genitals crushed. A child in school couldn't finish a lesson in history, of all subjects, and be free of the threat of a grown-up throwing him into a church and gassing him to death. That didn't merely have to change, as I saw it that day. Evolution was no good. It had to stop then and there. And my entire political life has been, and still is, founded, not on the rebuilding of a place that had rotted away, but on the making with my own hands of a method for humans to live, with just enough risk to stimulate them but not enough to kill one another.'

'Are you saying that something good came out of what I did?' Kestner said.

'How dare you suggest that?'

'Because I would like to believe it.'

'How dare you? I may say it perhaps. I experienced what little opportunity for good you and your swinish friends left behind you in Lascaud, but you are not to prop up the remains of your ego with any such assumptions of rectitude. Understood?'

'I am sorry,' Kestner said. 'You offer me friendship, which I at once betray.'

'Again that remark verges on self-pity, my friend. Nobody is helped by pity of any sort, least of all oneself.'

Lorion swilled the dregs of his burgundy, then spat it back into the glass. At once the glass was removed by the quaking hand of a waiter. 'Let me continue,' Lorion said, 'if only to make it quite clear that you have nothing to gain by public confession except other people's loss. When I saw those smoking ruins you left, when I hung over the body of what might or might not have once been my beloved sister, I coldly knew that in future I had no choice but to dominate a world in which such things could happen – the world's worst accidents are human beings themselves, you know. Of all living things we are the least adjusted to life. And we alone enjoy the pain of knowing it. And if you think I ought shortly to publish a slim volume of apophthegms, please do not worry. I am. I shall send you a copy. They are composed in exquisite French, because in Lascaud as children we had good teachers, who beat us if we allowed infelicities of language to sully the sacred accuracy of thought.'

'If I am not dead by then,' Kestner said, 'I look forward to receiving a signed copy.'

'I am sure that prospect will keep you alive.'

With ceremony, to excuse the insult of Lorion's final gulp of wine, another half-bottle was placed to hand. The waiter receded over the parquet. And suddenly Kestner could not believe that he was making any headway against this man's entrenched responses. He said, 'Have you really no feelings at all about what I've told you?'

'None. You are placing before me facts that were once intolerable. Those facts have changed, because I have long since digested them. Those facts, as they used to be, have helped to make me into the man I am. The ashes of my home town, yes, transformed me into a phoenix. The ashes, therefore, have disappeared.'

'But the memorial is still there,' Kestner said. 'You keep the wound open. Why are you trying to remind other people when you claim to have assimilated it yourself?'

'I am not debating with you, merely bringing new facts to your notice. They may assist in altering your somewhat hysterical conscience, which seeks not just to reopen wounds, but to relive the whole episode self-indulgently in all its bloody detail. No, I will put it to you in different terms. They are snobbish ones. They make me out to be superior to all those good people who pass Lascaud on holiday and come to mourn or gloat over the violence which you unleashed in my town. Well, friend, I am indeed superior, if in only two ways. I am one of the few whose home, whose entire life, background, school, church, childhood, first loves, were totally destroyed. I am also one of the even fewer who have made another life because of all that. If it hadn't been for you, I would have settled down as a decent honest farmer, perhaps a notary, even both if I had been sensible enough to marry the same excellent woman – but *I would still be there*.' He paused. 'As it is,' Lorion continued, 'I am on my way to high office, perhaps even to the presidency.'

'And you owe it to me?'

'No, I owe it to the difficult, heart-breaking, desperate inner use I made of your foul crime,' Lorion said between his teeth. 'And what use have you made of it?'

'I have come here to pay my debt,' Kestner murmured.

'All that means is that you have spent forty years of your life reliving one day of it, with less and less ability to absorb what happened on that one day. What's your profession?'

'I have a trade. I have built up my own business in a small way. I am a pork butcher. I married someone of whom I had time to become very fond and we had one daughter, whom you have met. It hasn't been a bad life.'

'Certainly not. It has been no life at all.'

'How can you say that to a dying man?'

'I must say what I consider to be true, and you may share my views if you will,' Lorion said. 'You surely don't think I shall tactfully try not to hurt you, because your doctor has made a diagnosis which you might easily prove to be faulty.'

'How?'

'Oh, by spitting out your poison, your boredom, and deciding to make a run for it. Outdistance your disease, whatever it is. A man is threatened, as a rule, only by himself.'

'I haven't much time left,' Kestner said, aware that he was risking a renewed attack on his self-pity.

'How long have they given you?'

'Two or three months perhaps.'

'Generous,' Lorion said. 'Most people only come to life on occasion. And you've got ninety days, each of which will certainly dawn and bloom and fade, each a chance for you to deepen and sweeten and open up – what a miracle to have the future so neatly defined, so containable! You should be pleased, my friend. The rest of us may die tomorrow without a word of warning. They did at Lascaud. That's just what happened, isn't it? Seven hundred people, like you, like me, woke that morning in various states of mind, from grumpy to blissful, but on the whole not displeased to be alive, hearing birds or taking no heed, sniffing roses or failing to notice that it was a fine sunny day, loathing the prospect of lessons or harvesting or housework, looking forward to coffee or bread or companionship and wine, a community of living bodies and souls over whom no threat hung and keeping to an age-old pattern that didn't attract threat. What a difference it must have made to them if they had been told that morning that they had three long and gorgeous months of summer, instead of just three innocent and unwarned hours! Do you still accuse me of having no feeling? Of having lost my love and admiration for that unsuspecting world, into which I was born and which you left for dead? Use your remaining time well, butcher. The only end you can safely predict is this minute, this second, as I finish these words – *now!*'

From a long way off footsteps were approaching the table with a large pot of coffee. Lorion had not ordered it; the waiters, long versed in his habits, discreetly knew his taste for quantities of coffee and when to time its arrival. To his own surprise Lorion now ordered some very old Armagnac dating from before the war.

'What kept me alive then,' he said, 'wasn't anger or the desire for revenge or pity for the wasted lives or any such transient and self-interested emotions. Not at all. Instead, as if sensing that my destiny was to become a statesman, I forgave everything. I taught myself to cooperate with the unthinking hatred I saw around me. I learnt to live easily with the idea of men, like yourself, so vilely tutored that they could excuse any horror by saying that they were under orders. I thereupon resolved to take orders from no one but myself. And I have never done so. You may call me arrogant. Many do. You may accuse me of an idealism so self-centred that at a superficial level it approximates to conceit. I ignore such charges. But what you can never say is that I have failed humanity, for the very simple reason that I do not believe humanity has so far given itself half a chance to start, let alone to exist, still less to be a continuous process that might in the end lead to some such glorious phase as civilisation.'

Lorion drew a cigarette case from an inside pocket. To prove his control of the habit he allowed himself the privilege of smoking once a day. He offered the cigarettes to Kestner, but they were of dark tobacco, not his brand. He took out his own. They shared a match, then smoked for a moment.

Inhaling so deeply that his head swam, Lorion said, 'The saddest thing on my sister's body, if indeed it were she, was a cigarette case blunted by a bullet which had probably entered her heart.'

Kestner grunted. His shoulders slumped. Lorion saw that his face was twisted in incomprehension, perhaps pain. The coffee cup, halfway to his mouth, clattered down into the saucer. He was motionless. The mirrors repeated him in their shadowy reflections: an elderly figure, at the end of a rich dinner, framed on the edge of life, perhaps falling, blood shuddering, heart giving out. The cigarette was burning close to his nails.

Lorion abruptly stood, trim as a soldier, snapped his fingers. From her desk the elaborate crone picked up the message and raised a hand loaded with rings. The last couple still dining stared, also frozen by the moment, a glass almost at the man's lips, the woman halting the dive of her spoon into a sorbet. A waiter behind a curtain registered the snap of fingers, the lifted hand of command, as they too were caught as if photographed in the infinity of mirrors. Mutely the waiter beckoned reinforcements from below. And still Kestner, the centre of the composition, did not move, though his jowls seemed to sag more, his limbs stiffen, his eyes glaze.

Nothing happened for a long moment, and then from silence footsteps echoed across the floor as if reviving a heartbeat, then in syncopation a more hurried rhythm of boots denting the stillness, and two waiters, both aged, were bent in dithering solicitude over Kestner, while Lorion, still standing, met the eye of the lady at the till, who nodded significantly towards the promise of a rear exit and pursed her lips.

And then with a deep sigh Kestner roused himself and said serenely, 'Oh, are we leaving?'

The man across the room returned to sipping wine. The woman swallowed sorbet. As ancient feet plodded back to the kitchens, the picture dissolved into the ordinary.

'What happened?' Lorion said in relief; death had entered this haven, then by a miracle receded.

'A fact,' Kestner said, 'upset me.'

'I talk too much,' Lorion murmured with a smile.

'I now know I did absolutely the right thing in demanding you and you only. Was your sister married?'

'Yes. Of course. Silly girl. She felt passion was all that mattered, so she fell for the first pair of trousers which she thought believed in it.'

'Who was that?'

'A good friend of mine,' Lorion said amicably. 'A prefect now. Down in the Gard. Socialist, of course – we had the same training in post-war politics, thanks to you. You left us quite a heritage, you know.'

'What did he do in the war?'

'Looked after a pâtisserie and killed Germans.'

'What was he like?'

'Bernard?' said Lorion, folding the bill. 'He was young like the rest of us. Sincere, foolish, vulnerable – what do you want me to say? In love with his wife, my sister. Wanting children. Ambitious to be more than a baker. If you were wondering whether you killed him, the answer is obviously no. He's a big man now.'

'And,' Kestner said, 'your sister was called Jeanne?'

'How do you know?'

'I loved her.'

Only a tightened mouth indicated Lorion's shock at the vulgarity of this statement. 'What do you mean?' he said.

'I am only here because I loved your sister, who is the only person I have ever loved.'

'Prove merely that you knew my sister,' Lorion said sharply.

'Believe me.'

'I may or may not believe you. I also want proof.'

'How can I? Oh, yes, I can describe her.' Kestner's tone was almost light in the flush of discovery that he could plunge the knife of truth into this man, who had found so many ways of rejecting the confession which had cost Kestner such efforts to make. 'Well, she didn't have any identifying mole on her left breast, did she?'

'My God,' said Lorion in a dispirited whisper.

'Sorry, but do you remember her bedroom? Yes, Bernard's bedroom too. The pattern on the wallpaper – of tiny roses, pink, but it was peeling off round the door. Is that proof? And the room smelt sickly sweet because someone had spilt a bottle of eau-de-cologne on to the white rug under the dresser that had family photographs on it in iron frames and there was a white counterpane on the bed which your grandmother had worked and just after five in the morning the room began smelling of bread from the bakery below. Enough?'

'I know you are not inventing this,' Lorion said. 'But how can you say it? To me of all people?'

'Only because it's true.' Kestner finished his glass of Armagnac. 'Hasn't the truth got some right to make itself known? Does it matter when or how it happens, provided it does happen? You can't blame either me or yourself for your ignorance of certain facts – which might have changed your life if you had known them earlier. They changed mine. In my heart I have been faithful to Jannie for nearly forty years. I didn't want to marry her or live with her or cope with her passions and watch them die into disappointment. I wanted to have her, or at least my own idea of her, for ever. She's much better dead. Is Bernard happily married now? I hope so.'

Breathing out a long sigh, Lorion occupied his fingers for several seconds with tucking the bill into his wallet.

'I know how you feel when you hardly know what to think,' Kestner said kindly. 'So think nothing. Feel what you feel.'

'I want no advice,' Lorion said.

'How would you have responded if you had known these facts, I mean about me, in 1944?'

'I would have discovered your name – what is it, by the way?'

'Ernst Kestner.'

'And I would have ransacked your country until I found you. Is it a common name? Never mind. I would have run you to earth in the end. Were you in the French sector?'

'The British. In Lübeck.'

'Thomas Mann's city,' Lorion said. 'A great writer. All the allies were looking for men like you who could prove by their continuing existence that we hadn't imagined the horrors you perpetrated. And then I would have brought you to justice.'

'Not killed me? In my own street? Or in bed?'

'Oh, no, no, no. Only the subtler forms of revenge have any sweetness. Humiliation. The slow breaking of a man in public. Ruining him for the rest of his life.'

'And is that what you intend to do now?' Kestner asked almost hopefully.

'Your name again?'

'Kestner.'

Putting two fingers abruptly to his forehead, Lorion closed his eyes, let his thoughts rest for a moment, then stared. 'I've got it,' he said with a snap of elation. 'Of course I could have located you. On the tenth of June, 1944, you, Ernst Kestner, and how could I forget, wrote a postcard to a woman in Germany coldly informing her that on your return after the war, if you survived, you would not be standing by your offer of marriage. Am I right? You phrased it like a legal document, didn't you? To conceal the guilt, I suppose.'

'How do you know this?'

'I have recently written a book about Lascaud. It may lack the turgid eloquence of your Thomas Mann, but as I said earlier I haven't lost the arts that a village school was humbly able to teach – clarity of thought, accuracy as to emotion, simplicity in style. In the archives of the Hôtel de Ville we discovered – my wife was helping me – the contents of the post-box at Lascaud recovered after the fire from the ruins of the building, put away in a thick sealed envelope in case anyone claimed them, unregarded for thirty years or more. Your postcard, with your name on it as sender, was there. It had not been collected. By the time the box was due to be emptied that Saturday afternoon, my friend, none of the people of Lascaud was in any position to communicate with anyone, except the divine power. And as proof that our enemies didn't in their usual inhuman way manage to think of everything, that there were human chinks in the armour of their totally anonymous assault on our town, I reprinted your postcard in my book – perhaps also in the hope that it might jog a memory and bring someone forward to offer new evidence.'

'It has,' Kestner said.

'No.'

'Not directly, perhaps. But I wouldn't be here if I hadn't written that postcard. Or been in love with your sister.'

In a heavily tired voice Lorion said, 'It is time we left. I haven't finished with you for the simple reason that I don't know where to begin. But you are still my guest tonight.'

'I will be, as they say in prison-camps, treated well,' suggested Kestner, again with the desire to undermine this man's apparently effortless capacity to take every shock in his stride.

'Assume nothing,' said Lorion with a faint smile. 'I may jeopardise my political future by having you garrotted. But it's too late for the ancient propriety of such gestures – you people proved that by doing much worse. No, I try to ape the kind of civilised man who I like to think will cleanse the future and make it safe for creatures like my sister to express the full extent of their passionate natures without recourse to the artificial stimulant of risk. That was it, wasn't it? You weren't in love. You merely played, as nations do when their spirits rise, the stupidly easy game of destroying each other.'

'We were in love,' said Kestner, standing upright.

Lorion also stood and began to lead the way out. Observing if briefly the courtesies to staff and management alike, the two men passed between the mirrors at a steady tread, as if curiously kin in all the repeated images of these old saloons.

Without another word they returned to the Renault parked outside. Kestner noticed that the night was clear. It occurred to him that the old burden had been lifted at last and placed squarely in the silence of another man's life. He need bear it no more.

Meanwhile he began to enjoy the ride. Lorion drove soberly through the outskirts of Celles, well under the limit. Cafés were closing down the long thoroughfare that dimmed at the last street-lamp into countryside. He switched on headlights, but the moon was strong enough to open the road in front of them. The swish of tree-trunks measured their accelerating speed. Kestner looked out sideways with satisfaction at the moon intermittently blinded by foliage. Farms shone faintly at a remove. Sweeps of field were phosphorescent in harvest under the stippled purple of the sky.

'Have you been there at night?' Lorion said without warning.

'Where?'

Lorion sighed.

'It's dark,' Kestner said in nervous protest. 'What could you see?'

'There's a full moon.'

And then, instead of fear, an excitement possessed Kestner, a closeness: he and this unshakeable man were setting out on adventure together. Had anyone dared visit the ruins of Lascaud at night since the street-lamps went out forty years ago? The prospect lay beyond thought, almost beyond possibility. Yet here they were with resolution following a signpost down the curves of a country lane, moths breaking cover from the umbelliferous depths of the hedges, the moon changing quarter at each turn of the wheel. 'There it is,' Lorion said, and between the trees Kestner caught a suddenly illuminated glint of glass under the swing of the moon, and in seconds they had drawn up under the high-windowed wall of the church. The busy silence of the cicadas of a summer night fell.

Kestner shivered. They stood together for a moment listening to the only modern sound, the click of the engine cooling in the warm night. A spray of white roses dropping over a wall grew luminous as their eyes took in the architecture outlined by the moon. Then Lorion stepped briskly off down a well-known alley past the church and they emerged into the uneven space in front of the north door, where along the street roofless shadows crowded in a zigzag of black. The silence appeared to deepen, if only because neither man spoke.

The moment was very heavy. Kestner felt an unbelievable unacceptability in the fact of his own presence. What was there to see behind the blind beauty of the night? Then he whispered, 'They are still here.'

Lorion, very close, but as if absent, said nothing.

'Yes,' said Kestner, to confirm his view.

Yes, he believed this then; it was all he believed. Even if Lorion were engineering solemnity for some purpose of his own, the weight of death was so intense that it could only be felt as life. Afterlife? Here, exactly here, he had shot this man's sister whom he had loved and still loved. No pause was long enough to realise the implacability of that fact. Among the repetitive mottoes of nature at night, the nightingales agonising

III

the silence, traffic from a faraway road, he was almost holding her, hearing her catch her breath. But then without a word Lorion, as if impatient to move further into the unknown, strutted off eagerly towards the Champ de Foire which, with its memories of lorries descending, children hastily summoned from school, mothers washing up the remains of lunch, notaries snatched from a minor point of law, farmers caught napping, all the nice balance and business of a society on a Saturday afternoon pursuing gentle ends, lay now in a flood of ever brightening moonlight. A single wall with nothing behind it stood for the hotel, out of which those eating good food in order to prolong life had been fetched to have life inelegantly terminated. Through the rough embrasures of what were windows of once comfortable bedrooms shone slants of the moon. And at last Kestner could feel the fear.

The fear, as if his own, racked his body. The moon swam in his eyes. As if itself alive, the fear caught his breath. Fingers pressed into his ribs. A tightening pain clutched the underpart of his heart. 'They are still here,' he whispered again, wanting to believe it.

'Yes,' Lorion said aloud. His voice was pitched high enough to silence nature for a second, then again the night began susurrating in corners of the square. Kestner felt his spirits dispersing. 'So what I want to do,' Lorion said, knocking a flat echo from the façades with nothing behind them, 'is to pull this place down and forget it. It's no longer a memorial but a burden. Frenchmen come here as tourists to relieve themselves of responsibility, to wallow in a past which they no longer value, to assert their right to stop thinking about the future. I have the power,' he said, raising his voice as if to convince an audience, 'I have the power to deprive Europe of this stupid memorial to stupidity. Tomorrow morning, without consulting anyone, I bring in my demolition men and raze to the ground this singular act of hostile piety.'

Lorion paused, as though for peroration. 'You are still here, says my friend. Yes – you are. But now you will be free. And then we too can break away from this petty old reminder of the violence which we all once shared.'

Kestner felt a hand round his shoulder, his cheek grazed on stubble, his arm went up, his chest bumped against a rib-cage, the sequence was repeated for the other cheek, and the embrace was over. And in that sudden moment's forced emotion he felt angrily bereft of a past that had kept him company for forty years; and tomorrow, when the bulldozers started up, would leave him finally alone.

Lorion turned and walked swiftly away to the car.

His hands were loose on the wheel and Lorion tried not to think in the car, but he thought.

There was no traffic to mock or challenge him on these country roads. The farms were long abed. He had no witnesses to any action he chose to take, save this doomed figure seated beside him, who for weeks had violated Lorion's sister only to stand back at her killing and watch it, which was worse than killing her by his own hands in bed, when she must have often wanted, as Lorion knew so well, to tighten her hands at his throat in her moments of foully vicious climax, because she as a younger girl had shared her brother's love of risk, of taking off from home, the pair of them, before the war, but making their own war out of the loose summery peace of the place where they were born, taking off into the woods, swerving this way and that to avoid the unseen enemies of the myths they invented together, hiding in hollow trees to jump out at each other on a long scream, making up tales of the cruel giants whose ghosts flickered with the kingfishers along the rivers, and ending up panting, all alone and far from the town, enjoying not daring to touch each other, each looking into the other's similarly shaped eyes, then climbing into cleft branches to eat cherries by the handful, juice bloodying their chins, the fruit of these same families of farmers who had turned off their lights: witnesses then, as now, of nothing that Lorion might choose to do.

Yes, surely then she must have wanted to kill this German, at just the moment when she was weakly taking most pleasure out of his body, when he was invading her with his foreign strength, her hands clenched round his throat in that last tight orgasm, before next day he allowed her, without identifying himself, part of a cruel giant, to be murdered.

At that moment Kestner awoke from a doze thinking that his host had fallen asleep. He nudged him hard with an elbow. And then the car was careering along the edge of a long open road, the nearside tyres shearing off the verge. At an angle it bumped abruptly off a bank of long grasses, which reared into the windscreen then fell away as the car, momentarily under control, swerved back into the middle of the empty highway, zigzagging along the unmarked crown for perhaps a hundred metres.

But it was evident that Lorion was not asleep. His profile was firmly set in the light dimly cast back from the road, and his eyes gleamed as he tried to correct the car's error. The speedometer read 150. Kestner let the speed, the feel of the risk in his body, flood through him like pleasure.

The accident – there was no call for it, no traffic, no sudden bends – was almost beautifully precise; even with irony, since anyway he was dying, Kestner had plenty of time to appreciate the clarity of its slow motion, as if he had caused it by the sudden panic of his own waking up. Out of the corner of his eye he registered Lorion, whose shoulder jammed against him, in the act of righting a fault in steering, a bit too much acceleration, braking a split second too late. And then they had mounted a bank, cleared it by inches as if flying, and were hurtling towards a clutch of trees. Branches crunched into metal overhead. The car tipped bottom over top and landed upright with a jarring bump, bouncing once, twice, then again on its tyres, in a field of ripe barley up to the windows a good way off the road.

At final impact Kestner's head struck the windscreen, smashing it into a star of glass that briefly blinded him, but he could smell blood and oil, intimately, in rising fear, and then in an elongated moment a loud hot puff breathed round him and the back of the car burst into a torrent of flame.

Kestner opened his door, fell out. A pack of moths dithered in the luminous air. He felt his legs slowed by acid green bindweed snaking through the corn, poppies glared. He rounded with an effort the car's bashed front, wrenched open the driver's door with fire in his face, and pulled out into the depths of the barley, already aflame, the body, still writhing, alive, of the brother of the only woman he loved. And with joy. He was aware of delight. On his tongue he tasted the blood coming from his own head. And it seemed now that he was saving from death the remnants of what mattered to him.

In seconds the car would go up. But he had survived; he had saved someone. And just then, as he dragged Lorion back, the entire field of barley seemed to be consumed in blowing flames that blotted out the moon, until the car with an explosion filled the countryside with light.

When at Auzances the telephone rang below-stairs and the roar of motorbikes neared the house and threw swathes of light briefly across her ceiling, Tina was in bed. To her disbelief the English journalist was kneeling up to her, his torso erect, arms stretched as if crucified, dark mouth set in a rictus of pleasure. All evening she had sought with greed this high moment of relief from the day's tensions, and here was her father, at just the wrong moment, returning from his official confessions under armed guard.

For her the hours had passed in an increasingly romantic glow as the summer night darkened. It had all come pat: champagne against the sunset, nightingales plummy in the shrubberies counterpointing the fluid talk, dining within at a long table amid a gathering mostly of men, candlelight fluttering on polished wood, a choice of home-made terrines, the wild duck sliced thin, a local cheese that smacked of farmyards, the pick of the afternoon's raspberries, her body quickening under the journalist's whisper of compliments – and a solid sense that the day's horror was none of her business.

Then, deepening the tone of Tina's enjoyment, Louis Larguier sang one or two of his ambiguous ballads on the terrace and that led to dancing in the warm air, some whisky, a tranquil ache in the limbs. And now, hours later, guilt absent and the night still young, this William was beside her in bed – but suddenly with headlamps ranging over the frieze of cherubs, a roar in her ears, the telephone ringing on and on in the house that was supposed to be asleep.

'What's all that?' William said, his voice withdrawing.

'I expect it's my father.'

'That sounds convincing, but can't be true.' He paused. 'Xavier always spends his evenings out incognito. No escort, no security. It's madness, but that's his way.'

The telephone stopped. A doorbell rang. Then the phone started again and his body tensed next to her.

'Don't go,' she said.

'I must. Something has happened. This isn't normal. There's a story here.'

'Will you come back?'

'With any luck.'

He was putting underpants on. She grimaced in the silence that rang with loss, a solitary nightingale muted by the shutters – then downstairs a commotion, very brief. A door slammed in the passage, slippers flapping at speed on tiles. William, bent double, was nagging at his shoelaces. A wave of fear lifted into Tina's not quite satisfied body, as if she were being left. She heard the echo in the hall of a woman's scream, cut off hard.

'You just wait here,' he said.

'I must go to her.'

The telephone began again, and would ring on and off all night.

For three weeks Kestner barely spoke. First in intensive care – his burns were bad – he was allowed no visitors, and when after a week they wheeled him into a private ward only his daughter was permitted to sit with him for a short period daily. His face was invisible. She found nothing to say to it.

The doctors soon discovered the cancer. Though delicately aware of the expensive irony, they did not allow its presence to diminish their efforts to repair the damage done by the accident. Marie-Louise Lorion volunteered to pay the running costs of this bizarre race between death and life, Tina insisting that she would repay Xavier's estate the minute she inherited whatever her father was soon to leave her – at least the shop and house in Lübeck, perhaps some savings too. At this point, three days after the tragedy, the two women exchanged for the first time a smile, slight, wan, but touched with complicity, if not comfort.

'Stay as long as you like,' Marie-Louise said.

'I want to,' said Tina.

She assumed that on the fatal night, while she was making love, her father had told Lorion the entire story. Somehow the accident had sprung from that testimony, causing an unjust death. Her father's dying, soon to be welcomed, but welcomed for his sake, would close the incident for ever, leaving Tina with not only a full version of the facts, but the responsibility for never telling a soul. Her contentment here at Auzances, a promisingly sexual one, was strengthened by the loyal satisfaction that her father's secret was safe with her. She even relished the privilege of being the only person left to know. So exclusive a burden had the luxury of grief, but without the pain.

'You're happy,' said Marie-Louise.

'For once,' Tina said. 'It used to be only in fairy-stories or on other people's faces. I'm sorry . . .'

'Oh, don't apologise. It's a relief to be with someone who's happy. A reminder . . .'

So during these fine days Tina stayed on at Auzances. The weather held. Each day echoed the day before as if time were reminiscing. Dawns kept repeating sunsets at the opposite extremes of the sky. She sunbathed in uninterrupted corners of the estate while skimming her dead host's book about the subtler ideals for Europe which the end of the war had narrowly failed to forge. Only Lorion apparently had retained any grasp on them, and now he too was gone, killed – the last victim of that war. Tina joined Marie-Louise for an aperitif, then lunch, and she slept in the hot afternoons, awaiting the return from Paris of the prime cause of her happiness, who would sleep with her at night.

'You're in love with him,' said Marie-Louise.

'Yes, but he's not worth it,' Tina said lightly.

'Everyone's worth it. Even Xavier was.'

Tina stared.

'Living with him wasn't happiness, you know,' said Marie-Louise chattily. 'But it was life. It still is. What about your husband?'

'No.'

'Or your father? Some women . . .'

'I'm free of him now.'

'It's like a war suddenly ending. Good. Xavier's much easier to love now he's not an enemy. Everything that was good about him he's left behind.'

Tina, still staring, saw this woman almost in tears. Her eyes pricked with sympathy. Her father was as good as dead. But William was no longer here either – as enemy or friend. After staying a day at Auzances to draw material from the local drama produced by Lorion's death, he had been recalled to Paris by his London paper to report on the political disorder expected to break out. Not much did. At first the French newspapers were headlined with the loss to France, indeed to European unity, which the demise of Xavier Lorion might or might not represent. On television each channel fielded a team of experts, who nightly for a day or two obscured the implications of the event in partisan rage or relief dressed as regret. A right-wing paper, casting him in elevated metaphor as a political chauffeur under orders from the back seat, investigated Lorion's capacity and record (he had twice been fined for speeding) at the wheel of a car, thereby casting aspersions that were no longer pertinent on his ability to conduct a nation into the future. This was cheap. The left gravely honoured his memory, then abandoned him. That was even cheaper.

His dismissal from the scene was somehow too curt. After a week he might never have existed. William filed as many reports as he could justify before the material thinned, knowing how much more intimate an attack he might make on his subject if he returned to Auzances, but puzzled by his reluctance to contemplate the journey south. Certainly he did not want the German woman, if only because he had had her; that spoiled night had yielded enough of sex. Yet she could lead him to her father. With a few sweet nothings he telephoned her every day, but only to check whether Kestner had at last opened his mouth, or Marie-Louise had emerged from mourning into revelation, or Tina herself had remembered a fact which clicked into exclusive place the truth about the tragedy. But so far Tina had told him only that she and her father had been on holiday together.

Just one newspaper, at the pinkish centre of the spectrum, had discovered (but how?) and printed (with what motive?) the theory that Lorion in his plunge to death had been accompanied (why?) by an unknown German, late at night, in the vicinity of Lascaud-sur-Marn, the place where the Germans had last imposed on the French their least forgivable insult. Nobody else took this point up. And William began to wonder why not.

The London news-desk stopped pestering him for follow-ups. The man was dead; so was public interest. William booked his flight home. Then, supping up the last of Paris in a Montparnasse restaurant, at a hint from a drunk on a magazine who babbled about murder, William hurried to the phone, first to postpone his reservation, and on second thoughts, sensing in his cups the story of a lifetime, to cancel it.

Early next day, determined by that hint to finish his book on Lorion even at the risk of losing his regular job, William caught the morning train to Celles at the paper's expense. His only obligation was to the truth as he saw it, and by now he was distinctly suspicious of Lorion's brisk fade from public notice. The meanness of politics could not alone account for the brevity of the nation's grief. Who actually was this German? And what had he done to the Frenchman? In a reaction of fright to Tina's evident longing for his body, William delayed contacting her – though bowing to the inevitable – until he had taken a taxi to Lascaud and spent the afternoon conducting all the obvious interviews.

These were predictably futile, though in his earlier search for background he had been introduced by Lorion to the men he now questioned. A minor official called Domergue passed him hurriedly on to the Mayor's Secretary, one Bressac, who in turn referred him to the Chief of Police. William formed the impression that Domergue, who claimed never to have heard tell of any German, was scared of losing his job; that Bressac, who implied with hostility that any such enquiry was a sign of disrespect for the town's venerated dead, might know more, but was silenced by his adherence to values long outmoded; and that the Chief of Police, sincere only in his hatred of the press, was keeping his own counsel. That William was writing an authorised study of Xavier Lorion, a fact they well knew, only increased the bitterness of municipal mistrust. He was out in the cold.

But on ringing Marie-Louise Lorion from the café he was at once invited to stay, too warmly; in the background the German half of the act was positively cooing. Were these women in collusion? He had expected a solemn acceptance of his right to pursue his hero into posthumous investigation. But enthusiasm for his presence? Marie-Louise even sent a car to pick him up. And the two women greeted his arrival on that balmy evening with a quiet, almost coy lack of reservation, as if he were an illicit relief from a mourning that now irked them both. The German girl squirmed and flirted as they quaffed champagne as of old on the terrace. Over dinner they all discussed Xavier's qualities, determined, it seemed, to ensure on his behalf an obituary beyond his deserts – for already William, bereft of Lorion's charisma, was doubting his worth. And then Marie-Louise, as befitted a widow, went to bed early, complaining of, of all things, a headache. It looked like a set-up.

After a few minutes of staring into his eyes ('alone at last') Tina led him upstairs, suppressing the odd giggle, forcing him into an embrace on a landing under a Matisse, opening up her room with a wink, then, door locked behind them, flinging her body on to the counterpane in a riot of clothes half shed. And nine hours later, by some mishap, by his failure to put the questions properly or because he was too busy sleeping things off to hear the reply, William was no wiser. Tina had told him nothing of what he knew she must know.

For three and a half days William paid almost sleepless court to his German admirer. There was no escape. The household routines, once thrown into continuous flux by affairs of state, were all of a sudden dumbly adjusted to the passions of this woman. The weather worked for her; the days were hot, the nights soft. With decorum Marie-Louise Lorion kept to herself, providing meals and presiding at them, retiring at the earliest moment to leave the young lovers the freedom of the estate. A secretary or two continued to work at Xavier's papers, the last of his unfinished business. But the telephone rang less and the days grew hotter. Tina had put on a tan, her flushed skin became a matter of pride, she walked with a flourish. While in theory repelled, William kept being tempted by the idea of her body, in the hope of inducing her by caress to speak her mind. He knew he must love her, or give up the quest.

All Tina knew was that never before had she loved another human being. Against her wish her heart almost broke at the sight of him eating his breakfast. When he stood up she quailed. He always seemed to be far away, even when in the same room. His voice entranced her, his body drew her, his presence hurt like absence. Twice she had rung her husband first to confirm that Henri with typical lack of intuition had failed to connect her father with the fuss in the newspapers, then to say that she was attending her father in hospital after a minor accident. Henri's fury at the domestic inconvenience struck her as so selfish as to prove her love for someone else.

For her, William, at last, was a man. His glasses, his floppy hair, the pimple on his neck, his soft belly, his shying away from her when she touched him by chance, his coming back to her from Paris, his nose, convinced her. And he loved her in return. Surely. He kept questioning her about her life. Was her childhood happy? Was she? And also asking after her father. Was he on the mend? Had he started talking? At every dusk – she visited hospital in the late afternoon – she repeated a blithely negative answer to William's questions, and this daily setback seemed for no good reason to renew his energies. With a groan he would take her to bed, rashly, lying with her before dinner in the sultry light filtered through the dead air of the heat-wave. At such moments he wanted to kill her.

And then on his fourth day Tina said unprompted, 'I told my father you were writing a book about Xavier Lorion. I don't know why, but he wants to talk to you.'

'Er . . .' William hardly knew what to say. 'I mean, is he fit enough?'

'No.' She sounded sprightly. 'He'll probably be dead tomorrow.'

'When can I see him, then?'

'Tonight? Before we . . .'

'Does he speak English?'

'No.'

'French?'

'Not really.'

'Then I won't understand him,' William said.

There was a pause. The remorseless summer hummed beyond the shutters as Tina rolled naked out of bed with a smirk.

'I can translate what he says.'

'It won't be the same.'

'It'll be better,' she said, 'because I love you.'

His back to her, William pulled on his underpants.

An hour later Kestner was sitting up in bed, much bandaged. His mouth showed. It smiled and began speaking. William waited, pen in hand. The crude syllables continued to emerge in just above a whisper from Kestner's lips, though his eyes were blinded by folds of dressing. Tina listened, nodding, took his hand, pressed it, frowned, kept nodding, put her hand to her brow, pursed her lips, kept track. Then she said, 'My father says that the night before he left Lübeck to start his journey he was awoken in the small hours by the next-door dog.'

'Really?'

'For some reason the poor fellow had been left out in the garden,' Tina said.

'Is this relevant?'

'And that was the day my father was leaving for France.'

The story had begun. William's notebook was on his knee. For a moment he wished he could understand the man's language, but did it matter? At the very least the narrative involved the death of a future president. The truth would make his name, unless the witness died before he could get all his lies down on paper.

'Go on,' William said.

'That's all so far,' Tina said spitefully.

Kestner had fallen asleep.